Temple felt Clin[...]
on the ground.

"What the—" he said, trying to get up. Only then did he realize there had been a shot.

"Stay down!"

"What the hell happened?"

"Someone took a shot at us."

"Us?"

"Me," Clint said. "You. Come here."

He pulled Temple across the street, where they took cover behind a horse trough.

"Where did it come from?"

"I don't know," Clint said. "It's too dark."

"Why don't you have your gun out?" Temple asked. "Isn't that what gunfighters do at the first sign of trouble? Draw their gun?"

"Not if they don't know what to shoot at," Clint said.

DON'T MISS THESE
ALL-ACTION WESTERN SERIES
FROM THE BERKLEY PUBLISHING GROUP

THE GUNSMITH by J. R. Roberts

Clint Adams was a legend among lawmen, outlaws, and ladies. They called him . . . the Gunsmith.

LONGARM by Tabor Evans

The popular long-running series about Deputy U.S. Marshal Custis Long—his life, his loves, his fight for justice.

SLOCUM by Jake Logan

Today's longest-running action Western. John Slocum rides a deadly trail of hot blood and cold steel.

BUSHWHACKERS by B. J. Lanagan

An action-packed series by the creators of Longarm! The rousing adventures of the most brutal gang of cutthroats ever assembled—Quantrill's Raiders.

DIAMONDBACK by Guy Brewer

Dex Yancey is Diamondback, a Southern gentleman turned con man when his brother cheats him out of the family fortune. Ladies love him. Gamblers hate him. But nobody pulls one over on Dex . . .

WILDGUN by Jack Hanson

The blazing adventures of mountain man Will Barlow—from the creators of Longarm!

TEXAS TRACKER by Tom Calhoun

J.T. Law: the most relentless—and dangerous—manhunter in all Texas. Where sheriffs and posses fail, he's the best man to bring in the most vicious outlaws—for a price.

THE GUNSMITH

397

LET IT BLEED

J. R. ROBERTS

JOVE BOOKS, NEW YORK

THE BERKLEY PUBLISHING GROUP
Published by the Penguin Group
Penguin Group (USA) LLC
375 Hudson Street, New York, New York 10014

USA • Canada • UK • Ireland • Australia • New Zealand • India • South Africa • China

penguin.com

A Penguin Random House Company

LET IT BLEED

A Jove Book / published by arrangement with the author

For information, address: The Berkley Publishing Group,
a division of Penguin Group (USA) LLC,
375 Hudson Street, New York, New York 10014.

ISBN: 978-0-515-15500-6

PUBLISHING HISTORY
Jove mass-market edition / January 2015

PRINTED IN THE UNITED STATES OF AMERICA

10 9 8 7 6 5 4 3 2 1

Cover illustration by Sergio Giovine.

ONE

Harry Temple rode into the town of Abilene, Kansas, feeling the weight of a two-year hunt on his back. The saddle he sat on and the gun belt around his waist were worn. That was because they had once belonged to someone else. The trail clothes he was wearing still felt odd to him, not because they, too, had once been worn by someone else, but because he'd once dressed in very different clothes.

Temple was from the East. Born and raised in Philadelphia, he wasn't used to cowboy boots and gun belts. At least, he hadn't been until about two years ago, when he came west. This was a whole new Harry Temple, not the one who had spent his first thirty-two years in Philadelphia, and then several years working in Boston.

Over the past two years the man had changed drastically. Not just in the way he dressed, but the way he thought, and felt and acted.

He reined in his horse in front of the first saloon he came to and dismounted. After tying the horse to a hitching post among a few others, he entered the place and found himself a spot at the crowded bar.

"Beer," he said to the bartender.

"Comin' up." The bartender's hand dwarfed the mug he

set down in front of Temple. He was a big, meaty man in his forties. "There ya go."

"Thanks."

Temple heard some raised voices in the back of the saloon and looked that way, as did the others at the bar. There was a crowd of men back there, watching some activity or another.

"Passin' through?" the bartender asked.

"Yeah, that's what I'm doing," Temple said. "What's going on back there?"

"Poker game."

"High stakes?"

"Not really."

"So what's all the fuss about, then?"

The bartender leaned his massive forearms on the bar.

"It's who's playin'."

"And who's that?"

"The mayor, the district attorney," the bartender said, "a couple of local ranchers."

"Doesn't sound like a whole lot to attract a crowd like that."

"There's one more player in the game."

"And who's that?"

"Clint Adams."

Temple paused with his mug halfway to his mouth.

"The Gunsmith?"

"The same," the bartender said.

"Well, friend," Temple said, "where I come from, that's called burying the lead. Maybe it's worth taking a look. Thanks."

He took his beer and walked to the rear of the saloon.

There were five men around the table, as the bartender had said, and they weren't hard to identify. The best dressed of them, a big, florid-faced man, had to be the mayor. Another man wearing a suit, a few years younger—with his jacket hanging on the back of the chair and dark sweat rings soaking his white shirt beneath his arms—had to be the district attorney. Two other men, both in their fifties, wearing clean ranch clothes, had to be the ranchers.

That left the fifth man.

Clint Adams.

Tall, wearing trail clothes that were worn but not old, he also seemed to have most of the chips in front of him. He sat, calmly looking at his cards, while the other men made their plays, and then he tossed some chips into the pot. While Temple watched, more times than not, he also raked in the pot.

Temple nursed his beer while he watched the game progress. An idea was forming in his head, and he wanted to let it roll around awhile, as he always did. He prided himself on never jumping the gun, and always giving situations enough thought. He'd done that even with the decision he'd made that had backfired on him and sent him out here to the West. And even so, he didn't completely regret it.

The people around him changed positions, as some left and new ones came. They weren't there to see the game as much as they were there to see the Gunsmith.

Temple could see the chips on the table, and from listening closely, he knew what the denominations were. They may not have been playing high stakes, but there was still hundreds of dollars on the table.

He asked a passing girl for another beer, and settled in to watch Clint Adams clean them all out.

TWO

While Temple nursed his second beer, people gradually lost interest as Clint Adams won three out of every four hands. Eventually the mayor and the district attorney tapped out and quit, leaving only Clint Adams and the two ranchers. From the conversation, it soon became clear that Adams was friends with one of the men; maybe they'd known each other before he came to town.

"I've had it," the other rancher said. "Thanks for the poker lesson, Adams."

"My pleasure, Mr. Blake," Clint Adams said. "Anytime."

The rancher stood, shook hands with Adams and the other man, and left.

Clint Adams looked up and saw Temple standing there.

"You looking for a game?" he asked.

"Me?" Temple said. "No, sir. I'm no gambler. I was just passing through, saw the crowd, and stepped up to see what the fuss was."

"Lot of fuss over nothing, if you ask me," Clint Adams said.

"You're too modest," the other man said. He was older, with the gray hair and wrinkles to go with the years. "What's your name, son?" he asked Temple.

"Harry Temple."

"My name's Abraham Corman," the older man said. "This is Clint Adams."

"I know that," Temple said. "Nice to meet you, Mr. Adams. You, too, Mr. Corman."

"Well," Corman said, "I better get on home. My wife's gonna be waitin'. Clint, you want to come to dinner?"

"Thanks, Abe, but I think I'll just stay in town tonight, spend some of my winnings on a steak and beer."

"Suit yourself. Make sure you stop by before you leave Abilene, though."

"You know I will."

Corman left while Clint Adams collected his chips and went to cash them in.

Temple took his beer back to the bar.

"Another one?" the bartender asked.

"No," Temple said, "I think I had enough. You can answer a question, though."

"What's that?"

"Clint Adams," Temple said. "Any idea how long he'll be in town?"

"Not sure," the barman said. "He came to town like you, just passing through. Found out he knew Abe Corman."

"Any idea how long he's staying?"

"I don't know that either. Why?"

"Just curious."

Temple turned and looked around the saloon. Clint Adams had collected his money and left.

"Any idea where I can get a good steak?" he asked the bartender.

"Now, there I can help you," the bartender said. "Go across the street and two blocks west to Jake's Steakhouse. Best in town."

"Thanks. What do I owe you?"

"Two bits," the barman said. "First beer was on the house for a first timer."

Temple dropped two bits on the bar and said, "Thanks."
He turned and left the saloon.

As he entered Jake's, he saw Clint Adams sitting at a back table, working on a beer and probably waiting for that steak he'd mentioned.

"Take any table," a waiter said as he passed. The place was busy, tables occupied by couples, families, and some lone men.

He started across the room to a table, but his attention was attracted by Clint Adams waving at him.

"Why don't you join me, Mr. Temple?" he asked.

Temple looked around, then walked over to Clint Adams's table.

"Don't mind if I do," Temple said.

"I ordered a steak," Clint Adams said. "Supposed to be the best in town."

"That's what I heard."

"From the bartender?"

Temple nodded.

"Me, too."

The harried waiter came over and took Temple's order, brought him a beer.

"Seems like you did pretty well at the game," Temple commented.

"I hope that doesn't mean you can't pay for your steak," Clint Adams said.

"I can pay," Temple said, "don't worry about that. But I'm curious about something."

"What's that?"

"Why would a man like the Gunsmith invite me, a stranger, to eat with him?"

"Maybe it's because I want to find out what that stranger wants with me. You got something on your mind, mister. What is it?"

THREE

Clint had been in Abilene for several days. Intending only to pass on through, he'd spotted someone he knew on the street. Turned out Abe Corman owned a ranch nearby, invited Clint out to see it and have a meal, so his one-day visit stretched out some.

The poker game in the saloon had started innocently enough among Clint and some other patrons, but soon the mayor joined in, and then the district attorney, and finally Corman entered the saloon with another rancher, and they joined the game.

When the word got out that the Gunsmith was playing poker, it attracted some crowds, which Clint was not pleased about. But he enjoyed poker very much, especially when he was winning, so he continued playing, and eventually, the novelty wore off.

Except for one man, who got a second beer and kept watching . . . and then walked into the same restaurant . . .

"What makes you say that?" Harry Temple asked.

"You spent a lot of time watching a poker game being played by a bunch of people you didn't know," Clint said.

"And you seemed real interested in me. I'll bet you even asked the bartender about me, which is why you're here."

"Well, you're right," Temple said, "I did ask him about you, but then I asked him about a good meal and he sent me here. I didn't know you'd be here."

"Then it's a coincidence," Clint said, "although I don't much believe in those."

"As a matter of fact . . ." Temple paused as the waiter appeared with their steaks. Both men leaned away from the steaming plates as their server set them down, almost expecting them to end up in their laps.

"You happen to be right," Temple finished when the waiter was gone. "When I rode into town, I had no idea you were here. Once I found out, I got interested."

Clint cut into his steak, saw that it was almost perfectly cooked. He was able to cut the potatoes and carrots very easily with his fork.

"So what's on your mind?"

"I was a journalist in Boston—"

"I don't do interviews," Clint said, interrupting him. "It's a rule of mine."

"Let me finish, please."

"All right," Clint said. "Sorry. Just wanted to get that out there."

"Up to two years ago I was a journalist in Boston," Temple said. "Then everything changed. There was a killer at large in the city. I got word from an informant about who it was. I checked with the police, and they asked me not to run the story."

"But you did."

"Like I said before," Temple answered. He had cut into his steak, but had not yet put any into his mouth. Clint chewed and waited. "I was a journalist."

"The story comes first, right?"

"That's what I thought."

"So what happened?"

"The killer left town."

"And the police held you responsible?"

"Hell, I *was* responsible," Temple said, "but it wasn't even that. They were just happy that he left Boston."

"But you weren't."

"No," he said. "If I had sat on my story, he might have been caught."

"So now . . . what? You're looking for him? Hunting him?" Clint asked.

"I heard stories about killings in Cleveland," Temple said. "But by the time I got there, he was gone. That was two years ago. And yes, I've been tracking him ever since."

"Tracking?"

"Well, I'm not a tracker, of course," Temple said, "but I've been following stories of cases that sound like him."

"What kind of cases?"

"He kills women, strangles them," Temple said. "But by the time I get there, he's always moved on." He shook his head, finally put a piece of meat in his mouth, but it didn't look like he was tasting anything. "He kills more women, and every one he kills is my fault."

Clint remembered dealing with stranglers in Oregon, New York, and London, England.

"I have some experience with those kinds of killers," he said.

Temple chewed more enthusiastically, but only so he could swallow and talk.

"Well, then," he said, "maybe you can help."

"How?"

"Come with me," Temple said. "Help me hunt him down."

Clint put another hunk of meat in his mouth and chewed thoughtfully.

"What brought you to Abilene?"

Temple took something out of his pocket. He unfolded it and showed it to Clint. It was a clipping from the *Abilene*

Reporter-News, the local paper. The story was about a woman being strangled.

"That was two weeks ago," Clint said.

"Took me two weeks to get here."

Clint handed it back.

"I've been here three days," he said, "haven't heard anything about it."

"You can help me, though," Temple said. "You have contacts here, and you can track."

"Contacts?"

"That rancher friend of yours."

"He's the only person I know in town."

"That's one more than I do," Temple pointed out. "I was just going to talk to the local editor."

"You can still do that."

"Yes, while you talk to your friend."

Clint chewed thoughtfully.

"Mr. Adams?"

"I can talk to my friend," Clint said, "but as far as tracking the killer . . ."

"Look," Temple said, "I'll take whatever help you can give me at this point."

"Yeah, okay," Clint said. "I'll do what I can—now eat that steak before it gets cold."

FOUR

They finished their steaks, had pie and coffee for dessert. When it came time to pay, they both dug into their pockets for money and paid for their own meals.

Out in front of the steakhouse, Clint said, "I've got to say you don't dress like a journalist."

"This?" Temple said. "Soon after I came to the West, I realized I needed to change everything about myself, including the way I dressed and traveled. So I bought these clothes, found somebody who would sell me their horse and saddle and gun belt."

"Yes," Clint said, "I noticed your rig was worn."

"I also did it because I needed to blend in, not stand out," Temple said.

"Well, you've done that," Clint said. "You don't look anything like a journalist."

Temple rubbed his hand over the stubble on his cheeks and said, "You think I can get a shave without ruining the look?"

"Sure, why not?" Clint asked. "Many a saddle tramp is clean shaven."

"Good," Temple said. This time he scratched his cheeks. "This was getting kind of itchy."

"Where are you headed now?"

"The newspaper office to talk to the editor," Temple said. "His name's Pete Tanner."

"Okay," Clint said, "you do that. I have a standing invitation out at Abe Corman's ranch, so I guess I'll take a ride out there and see what he knows about this murder of yours."

"It's not my murder," Temple said testily.

"Okay, sorry," Clint said. "I didn't mean anything by that."

"Yeah, okay," Temple said. "I don't have a hotel room yet, so I think I'll take care of that first."

"I'm staying at the Oak Tree Hotel down the street," Clint said. "I'm sure they have rooms."

"I'll try them."

"I'll check later to see if you got a room, and we can compare notes."

"See you then."

Temple headed down the street to the hotel, while Clint went the other way, toward the livery.

Clint collected Eclipse from the stable, welcoming the chance to have the big Darley Arabian stretch his legs.

He let the big horse gallop all the way from town to Abraham Corman's ranch, reining in the animal in front of Corman's house.

"Boss said you wasn't comin' out today," Ed Halston, the foreman, said as he walked over to greet Clint.

The two men shook hands and Clint said, "I didn't think I was, but something came up. Boss inside?"

"Yeah, he's at his desk," Halston said. "You want me to have your horse taken care of?"

"No, you can just leave him here," Clint said. "I don't think I'll be long."

"You want me to tie him off?" Halston asked as Clint

dropped Eclipse's reins to the ground. "So maybe he don't wander away?"

"No," Clint said, "that's good enough. He won't be going anywhere."

"Suit yourself," Halston said. "Come on, I'll take you inside."

"Lead the way."

They went up the white steps to the front door of the two-story house Abe Corman had built himself.

FIVE

Before they could get to Corman's office, they encountered his wife, Brenda, coming down the stairs from the second floor.

"Clint! How nice." She was a lovely woman in her early fifties, with a beautiful head of silver hair. "Abe told me you weren't coming out tonight."

"I wasn't, Brenda, but something has come up and I need to speak with him."

"Of course. I believe he's in his office . . . is that right, Ed?"

"Last place I saw him, ma'am."

"All right, then I'll take Clint to him."

"Yes, ma'am," Halston said. "See you later."

"Thanks, Ed," Clint said.

"Come on, Clint. Follow me."

She led him down a hallway to Abe Corman's office. The rancher was seated behind his desk, going over some paperwork.

"There he is," she said, "trying to cover the losses to you in poker."

"Quiet, woman!" Corman said with a grin. "Clint, what are you doing here?"

"I just need to ask you a few questions, Abe," Clint said. "I can't stay."

"The cook is making her famous rosemary chicken," Brenda said. "You sure I can't tempt you?"

"I'm sorry, Brenda," Clint said.

"All right, suit yourself," she said. "I'll leave you two to talk business, or whatever it is you're going to talk."

As Brenda left the office, Abe Corman said, "Have a seat, Clint. Tell me what's on your mind."

Clint sat across from his friend.

"It's about that young fellow who was watching us play earlier," he said.

"What was his name?"

"Temple," Clint said. "Harry Temple."

"Should that name mean something?" Corman asked. "I can't place it."

"No," Clint said, "it's not a name you'd know. Let me tell you what this is about."

"Go ahead," Corman said, "I'm listening . . ."

Several minutes later Corman nodded and sat back in his chair.

"Yes, I know about that murder."

"Why haven't I heard a thing about it since I got to town?" Clint asked.

"Well, as you know, I sit on the town council," Corman said. "It was the council's decision to keep the murder quiet. Keep it from being discussed on the streets and in the saloons."

"What will that accomplish?"

"We're thinking the killer might stay in town and try to strike again. Our police department is on alert."

"Who made this decision?"

"The mayor and the chief of police proposed it," Corman said. "The council approved it."

"Well," Clint said, "this fellow Temple seems to thinks

he knows who the killer is," Clint said. "He's been trying to track him for two years, and thinks he's the one who killed this girl."

"Then I suppose he'd better compare notes with the police so they can determine if he really is the same man," Corman said.

"Can you set that up?" Clint asked. "A meeting with the chief of police?"

"I can do that," Corman said. "Tomorrow soon enough?"

"That's fine," Clint said. "Temple and I will both meet with them."

"And if you don't mind, I'll be there."

"I don't mind at all," Clint said. "Now, can you tell me about the girl who was murdered?"

Clint left the Corman ranch after listening to everything his friend had to tell him. When he got back to town, he left Eclipse at the livery once again, went to his hotel to check and see if Temple had gotten a room. He had, but he wasn't there at the moment.

"Said he was going to the saloon," the desk clerk said. "Bet you can find him still there."

"Thanks," Clint said.

He left the hotel, crossed the street, and headed for the Big Horn, the same saloon where he'd first met the journalist, figuring that was the one he meant.

When he entered the saloon, he spotted Harry Temple at the bar right away, despite the fact that the place was—as always—pretty busy. The journalist was bent over a mug of beer, staring into it, apparently lost in thought. There was a man standing on his right, but the space was open on his left.

Clint bellied up next to Temple and said to the bartender, "Beer."

"That was a quick trip," Temple said, momentarily startled. "Did you manage to find out anything?"

"I did," Clint said. "A few things, in fact. What about you?"

"I did, too," Temple said. "The editor of the newspaper was very willing to help. Why don't we grab a table and compare notes?"

"Hang on. I just need to wash down some dust first," Clint said. He drank down the mug of beer and waved at the bartender for a refill.

"You want another one?" he asked Temple while he waited for his fresh one.

"No," the younger man said, "this is my second. That's usually my limit."

"Okay," Clint said when he had the fresh mug in his hand, "now let's sit and talk."

SIX

"You go first," Clint told him.

"Well," Temple said, anxious to talk, "when I left you, I went over to the paper . . ."

Temple entered the office of the *Abilene-Reporter News* and found it much larger than he had expected. The sounds of a printing press filled the air, and he could smell the ink. It immediately took him back to his time working on the *Boston Herald*.

"Help ya?" the man running the printing press asked. He was holding a white rag that was mostly black with ink. His fingers were also black, and he had smudges of ink on his face. He was tall, thin, in his forties.

"I'm looking for the editor, Pete Tanner," Temple said. "Is he around?"

"Pete expectin' ya?"

"I sent him a telegram."

"G'wan back, then," the man said. "Down that hallway to the end you'll find his office."

"Thanks."

Temple followed the hall back to an open door. Inside he saw a man writing at a desk, with his back to the door.

He knocked and said, "Mr. Tanner?"

The man turned. He was possibly the homeliest man Temple had ever seen, with buck teeth, freckles, and large ears. He was in his fifties, so his red hair was shot with gray.

"That's right," he said. "Pete Tanner. Can I help you?"

It was as if God had felt sorry for making him so plain looking, so he gave him a beautiful baritone voice.

"Yes, I'm Harry Temple." He saw no trace of recognition on the man's face. "I sent you a telegram? About the girl who was murdered?"

"Oh, yes!" the man said, slapping his hands together. "Sorry. I've got a lot on my mind." He stood up and shook hands. "You're the reporter from Boston."

"I was a reporter in Boston," Temple said, "but not for two years now."

"Wouldn't be lookin' for a job, would you?" Tanner asked. "I could use an experienced man like you around here."

"I'm sorry," Temple said, "I'm a little involved in something right now, so I'm not really looking for a job."

"Too bad," Tanner said. He sat back down, keeping his back to his desk. He folded his arms and regarded Temple quizzically. "What's on your mind?"

"You had a murder here a couple of weeks ago. A girl. She was strangled."

"What do you know about that?" Tanner asked, frowning.

"Not as much as I'd like," Temple said. "We had some stranglings in Boston. I'm trying to track down the man who did it, and I'm wondering if he's the same man who committed the murder here in Abilene."

Tanner hesitated, then said, "That what you meant by you haven't been a reporter for two years? You've been tracking him that long?"

"I have."

Tanner stroked his chin for a few moments, then stood up.

"You hungry?"

"I just ate."

"Me, too, but I could use a piece of pie. I know where the best pie in town is. You interested?"

"If I have pie with you, will you talk to me?"

"Pie and coffee," Tanner said, "and sure I will."

"Well, then," Temple said, "I'd love some pie."

"Come on," Tanner said, "we'll slip out the back way. It really annoys Billy out there when I disappear on him."

"Then why do you do it?" Temple asked.

"Didn't you hear what I said?" Tanner replied with a grin. "It annoys him!"

SEVEN

"He was right," Temple told Clint. "He took me to have the best pie I've ever had."

"You'll have to take me there," Clint said, "but finish telling me your story."

"Well," Temple went on, "like I said, we went for pie . . ."

"Laurie Wilson was just about the prettiest girl in town," Pete Tanner told Temple. "Had all the boys in town chasing after her with their tongues hanging out—half the grown men, too. At least, the ones under forty."

"Your story said she was eighteen."

"Just turned eighteen," Tanner said, nodding his head.

He had a piece of peach and blueberry pie in front of him. He tried to get Temple to try it. "Specialty of the house," he said, but Temple didn't like his peaches purple. He had a hunk of apple pie with his coffee.

"You know," Tanner said, pointing with his fork, "that apple pie tells a lot about you."

"Is that so? What's it say?"

"No imagination," Tanner said. "No adventure."

"If you knew what I've been through these past two years, you wouldn't say no adventure," Temple told him.

"No, you're probably right," Tanner said. "I'm sorry I said that."

"Forget it. The paper didn't say how she was killed."

"Sure it did," Tanner said. "It said she was strangled."

"It didn't say how," Temple said, "or with what."

"What makes you think it was with something other than a man's hands?"

"My guy uses an orange neckerchief," Temple said. "Leaves it behind, like a . . . a trademark."

Tanner put down his fork and sat back.

"Nobody in Abilene knows that except the police—and me," he said.

"So it was there?"

"Sure was," the editor said. "Right around her neck."

"Damn," Temple said, setting his own fork down.

But the two men didn't lose their appetites for long. They'd both been in the business long enough not to let that happen. They finished their pie and coffee and walked back to the office, going in the same way they'd come out—the back door.

They'd talked more, but the editor didn't have anything else to tell Temple beyond where the girl worked and lived.

"She worked at the general store," Temple told Clint, "right on Main Street. Lived above it."

"With anybody?"

"Nope, she lived alone."

"But she was eighteen."

"That's a grown woman, Clint," Temple said. "Both her parents died in an accident when she was twelve. She went to live with the family who owns the general store. When she turned eighteen, they gave her a room upstairs."

"How long had she been living there on her own?"

Temple looked at Clint and said sourly, "A week."

"Okay, well, look," Clint said, "nobody in this town talks about it because the word went out to keep it quiet.

And apparently when the chief of police and the mayor send out the word, folks listen."

"They're trying not to scare the killer off," Temple said.

"You got it," Clint said. "They want him to try again."

"Clint," Temple said, "it's been two weeks. He may already be gone."

"Well, you know," Clint said, "there's something you neglected to tell me."

"What's that?"

"You said you knew who this killer was," Clint said, "that you wrote it in your paper and that's the reason he left Boston."

"That's right."

"So?" Clint asked. "What's his name?"

Temple put his beer mug down and said, "His name's Daniel Mulligan." He stood up. "I'm getting another beer."

Clint didn't bother to remind him that he was already over his limit.

EIGHT

When Temple came back and sat across from Clint, he said, "Of course, that wasn't his real name."

"But it was the name he was known by in Boston."

"Yes."

"So you don't know what names he's been using during the past two years."

"I've actually gotten close to him a few times," Temple said. "There's one thing he can't seem to change."

"What's that?"

"His method," Temple said, "and the thing he leaves behind."

"Which is what?"

"I haven't told this to anyone but Pete Tanner, the editor," Temple said. "The killer uses an orange neckerchief to strangle his victims, and leaves it behind."

"Did you put that in the newspaper, as well?"

"No," Temple said, "but it didn't matter."

"What about the newspaper here?"

"No, they kept that out," Temple said. "Tanner said the chief of police threatened him if he put in the story."

"Well," Clint said, "I've arranged for you and me to talk

with the chief of police and the mayor tomorrow. And by that, I mean that Abe Corman arranged it."

"That's fine," Temple said, "but if you don't mind, I'd like to keep my background to myself for now."

"I don't blame you," Clint said. "They don't need to know the real reason you left Boston. But they do need to know that you've been tracking this guy for two years."

"'Tracking' is a grandiose word for it," Temple said. "I've been following a trail of bodies that he leaves behind him."

"What about the cities and towns you've been to where he took a victim?" Clint asked. "How did they treat you?"

"Nobody listens to what I say," Temple said. "For one thing, the murder has already happened. And if the killer has left town, that's all they care about. This will be the first time I get to actually sit down and talk to someone in authority."

"Well, then, we better make the most of it," Clint said. "What time is this meeting?"

"We'll find out in the morning," Clint said, "but we'll have to be ready. It might be first thing in the morning."

"Suits me," Temple said. "I'm about ready to turn in right now."

"I could do that, too," Clint agreed.

They stood up, left the saloon together, and headed for their hotel.

The shot came from out of nowhere . . .

Temple felt Clint's hands on him, and then he was rolling on the ground.

"What the—" he said, trying to get up. Only then did he realize there had been a shot.

"Stay down!"

"What the hell happened?"

"Someone took a shot at us."

"Us?"

"Me," Clint said. "You. Come here."

He pulled Temple across the street, where they took cover behind a horse trough.

"Where did it come from?"

"I don't know," Clint said. "It's too dark."

"Why don't you have your gun out?" Temple asked. "Isn't that what gunfighters do at the first sign of trouble? Draw their gun?"

"Not if they don't know what to shoot at," Clint said.

"Well," Temple said, "there hasn't been a second shot. Maybe the shooter is gone."

"One way to find out," Clint said. "Stay here."

Clint stood up warily, walked out to the center of the street they had been crossing when the shot came. He looked around on the ground, but it was too dark.

"What are you looking for?" Temple asked, coming up alongside him.

"I told you to stay put."

"There wasn't another shot," Temple said. "He's gone, right?"

"Looks like it."

"So what are you looking for?"

"A bullet," Clint said, "but it'll have to wait until daylight." He looked at Temple. "We'd better get off the street. Come on."

"Shouldn't we go to the police?" Temple asked, following along.

"We will," Clint said, "in the morning."

Clint left Temple in his room and went down the hall to his own. His window overlooked the street, and he stared out, wondering if the shooter was watching the hotel from the shadows.

NINE

Clint met Temple in the lobby the next morning.

"Any word on the meeting?" the ex-journalist asked.

"Nothing," Clint said. "Let's have breakfast here in the dining room, where they can find us."

"Suits me."

They went in, got a table, and ordered—steak and eggs for Clint, ham and eggs for Temple.

"Any thoughts about what happened last night?" Temple asked.

"Not really."

"Well, somebody took a shot at you."

"Or you."

"Now why would anyone shoot at me?" Temple asked. "You're the Gunsmith. Aren't you a more likely target?"

"What about the killer you're tracking?"

"I doubt he even knows I'm on his trail."

The waiter came with their plates, and they waited until he had set them down and withdrawn to continue their conversation.

"It had to be somebody shooting at you," Temple insisted.

"Maybe," Clint said. "I just don't like coincidences. I

mean, you're looking for a killer, and somebody takes a shot at us."

Temple was about to say something when he realized he'd lost Clint's attention.

Clint saw Abe Corman come through the door, look around, spot him, and head over. Even though he was already crossing the room toward them, Clint waved.

Clint stood and said, "Good morning. You remember Harry Temple?"

"Yes," Corman said, sitting, "he watched you beat my ass at poker."

"Yes, he did."

"Good morning," Temple said. "Thank you for agreeing to help us."

"I hope it's helpful to you," Corman said, "but I got you your meeting with Chief Landry and Mayor Stanley."

"Stanley?" Clint asked.

"Theodore Stanley," Corman said.

"Teddy," Clint said. "Last night you called him Teddy."

"Right," Corman said. "At the poker table, he's Teddy. Also, Ned Beaumont will be there."

"Ned," Clint said. "The district attorney." He poured Corman a cup of coffee, then went back to his breakfast.

"Right again."

"Anybody else?" Temple asked.

"Me."

"That's fine."

"Anybody else you want?"

"I only know one other person in town."

"Who?" Corman asked, sipping his coffee.

"Pete Tanner."

"The editor?"

Temple nodded and chewed.

"Not a good idea for him to be there."

"Agreed," Temple said.

"Where's the meeting?" Clint asked.

"City Hall."

"When?"

"As soon as you finish eating," Corman said, "I'll walk you over there."

"Something happened last night," Temple said.

"What?" Corman asked.

"Somebody took a shot at Clint."

"Or Harry," Clint said.

"Where?"

"On the street," Temple said.

Corman put down his coffee cup and looked at Clint.

"Who?"

"We don't know," Clint said. "It was dark."

"Well," Corman said, "it's not unusual for somebody to shoot at you, is it?"

"No," Clint said, "but it would be unusual if they shot at him."

"Who would shoot at you?" Corman asked Temple.

"Nobody."

"A killer," Clint said. "He followed a killer here."

"A killer? Who?"

"A man whose name used to be Mulligan."

"And what's his name now?"

"We don't know."

"And did he kill the girl?"

"That's what we want to find out," Clint said. He looked across the table at Temple. "Finished?"

Temple put the last bite of ham into his mouth and said, "Finished."

Clint ate his last chunk of steak and said to Corman, "Okay, we're ready. Lead the way."

"There's something you should know about the men you'll be meeting."

"What's that?" Clint asked.

"They're all very ambitious," the rancher said. "The mayor and the district attorney are politicians. The mayor wants to move up to the governor's mansion. The district attorney wants to be mayor."

"And the chief of police?" Clint asked. "What's he want to be?"

"Chief of police," Corman said, "for now."

"What's Landry's story?"

"Winston Landry," Corman said. "Every calls him Chief. A few people call with W.T."

"W.T.?" Temple asked.

"Wins-Ton," Corman said.

"Hmm," Temple said.

"He's tough, used to be a policeman in the East."

"Where?" Temple asked.

"New York."

"I'm from Philadelphia originally," Temple said. "I've probably known people like him."

"Well, then, maybe that'll help you get along," Corman said, "but I kinda doubt it."

"Why's that?" Clint asked.

"Because he's got his own way of doing things," Corman said, "and sometimes he rubs people the wrong way."

They all stood up.

"How did he get to be chief of police?"

"I think," Corman said as they headed for the door, "it's because he has his own way of doing things."

TEN

Clint and Temple followed Corman down to City Hall. They entered and he took them down a hallway to a closed door.

"This is the room where the town council meets," he told them. He knocked, opened the door, and led them in.

There was a long table that the council sat at during their meetings. It was long enough to seat eight men on either side, but on this day there were only three men in the room.

"Theodore Stanley, our mayor," Corman said, indicating the man seated at the head of the table.

The mayor nodded.

"Ned Beaumont, our esteemed district attorney."

Beaumont was seated at Stanley's right, as he had been at the poker table. Clint thought the DA was the mayor's right-hand man in more ways than one.

"Good morning, gentlemen," Beaumont said.

The third man in the room was standing, staring out the window to the alley. He turned slowly to face them. He had a sharp-nosed face with a scar down one cheek, a tall, fit, hard-looking man, to say the least.

"And this is our chief of police, Chief Landry."

Landry simply stared at the two men, then looked at Abe Corman.

"You're late," he said. "When I agreed to this meeting, we said nine. It's now five after."

"Well, I'm sorry about that, Chief," Corman said.

Clint knew Abe Corman pretty well. He knew that most people—men and women—ended up liking him after only a few minutes. The fact that he called the man "Chief" meant they weren't friends. Or he was just showing him respect in front of other people.

"But Mr. Adams and Mr. Temple are here now," Corman added.

"And they're here to help, W.T.," the mayor said. On the other hand, Clint knew that the mayor calling him W.T. was a politician's way of showing his superiority. It said, *We're not friends, but I can call you by your first name.*

"Have a seat, gentlemen," the mayor said. "We're anxious to hear what you have to say."

Clint and Temple took seats at the farthest end of the table, across from each other. Corman took a chair that was not near them or the others. Clint had a feeling it was where he usually sat at meetings.

The chief finally decided to sit down, across from Corman, staying separated from the mayor and his district attorney.

The townsmen waited and Clint finally nodded to Temple to go ahead and start. Temple told them about the murders in Boston and other cities, and how since the killer left and headed west, he'd been trying to track him.

"Why do you think you can catch this man when the law has not been able to?" the chief asked.

"I mean no disrespect to the law," Temple said. "I'm just trying to do my part."

"Bull!" the chief said.

"Chief," the mayor said warningly.

"This man is not telling us everything," the chief said.

"He's holding something back." The chief looked at Temple. "Tell us the rest of it, or I'm done here."

Temple looked at Clint, who could only shrug. It was up to the younger man if he wanted to tell them the whole story.

"I was working for the *Boston Herald* when this man was killing women there," Temple said, "and . . . I broke the story when I shouldn't have."

"Ha!" the chief said. "You alerted the killer and he left town, right?"

"That's right."

"So you're here out of guilt!" The chief sounded triumphant.

"You're right again."

"Ha!" the chief repeated.

"Chief," the district attorney said calmly, "I don't much care why the man is here, as long as he can help."

"I agree," the mayor said. "What do you think you have to offer us, Mr. Temple?"

"I have an understanding of how this man works," Temple said.

"Does that mean you think you can tell us when and where he'll strike again?" Ned Beaumont asked.

"I can sure as hell make an educated guess."

"So it's your belief the man is still in Abilene?" the mayor asked.

"I don't see why not," Temple said. "Up to this point he's seen no threat to himself."

"And that's because you don't work on our newspaper," the chief said, "so you can't write a piece that will warn him."

"Actually," Temple said, "the editor of your paper has offered me a job."

"No!"

"Don't worry," Temple said, "I didn't take it, but I am here to offer whatever help I can to catch this man."

"And you, Mr. Adams?" Beaumont asked. "What do you bring to the table?"

"Temple asked for my help," Clint said. "Admittedly, I'd be more help if the killer leaves town and has to be tracked down. But I'm like Temple in that I'll offer whatever help I can."

"I say we don't need their help," the chief said. "I can contact the police in Boston for whatever information they might have."

"And the police in Cleveland?" Temple asked. "And Chicago? And Saint Louis? And Oklahoma City? I've been to all those places and more—after the fact. This is the closest I've come to the killer."

"I think we'd be fools to waste this man's expertise," Beaumont said, looking at the mayor.

"I agree," Mayor Stanley said. "Chief, I'd like you to take these fellows over to police headquarters and work with them on this. We need to catch this killer before he leaves town."

The chief grumbled, and finally said, "As you wish, Mayor Stanley." He glared at Clint and Temple. "You fellas can come over in about a half hour. Just give me time to get settled in my office this morning."

"Whatever you say, Chief," Clint said.

The chief grumbled again, got up, and left the room.

"He's kind of ornery," the mayor said, "but he's good at his job."

"We'll just do what we can to help," Clint said.

The mayor stood up and shook hands with both Clint and Temple.

"We'll appreciate whatever you gents can do." He looked at Corman, who also stood. "Good to see you, Abe."

"Mayor."

The rancher left the room with Clint and Temple, leaving the mayor and the district attorney alone.

Outside in the hall Temple said, "The chief's not going to be an easy man to work with."

"Just give him a chance," Corman said. "He may come around."

"Abe, you'll show us where the police department is?" Clint asked.

"No problem," Corman said. "Come on."

Inside the room, Ned Beaumont looked at Mayor Stanley.

"What do you think?" Beaumont asked.

"I think what I've always thought," Stanley said, "only more so now. If we can catch this killer before he moves on and kills again, it'll be a feather in our caps—both yours and mine."

"I agree."

"So I think we should take whatever help comes our way."

"And," Beaumont said, "maybe if the Gunsmith stays around, we can get some of our money back at the poker table."

ELEVEN

When Clint and Temple entered the police station—a brand-new three-story brick building—they were immediately escorted by a policeman to a room much like the one they'd been in earlier, only with a smaller table. This one could have accommodated three men on either side.

"Somebody will be in to see you soon," the policeman told them.

"The chief, right?" Temple asked.

"I don't know," the man said, and left.

Temple looked at Clint.

"He must have someone, a detective, working on this," Clint commented. "Maybe that's who we're waiting for."

"Well, that'll suit me," Temple said. "He didn't strike me as the easiest man to work with."

"No, me neither."

Clint walked over to the one window in the room and glanced out. He found himself looking down at the roof of the building next door, which had only one floor.

"They could have offered us some coffee," Temple said.

"Hey," Clint said, turning away from the window, "they let us in the building. Let's start with that."

"You're right."

They heard footsteps coming down the hall outside the room. It sounded like a herd of buffalo, but only one man entered the room. However, he was so large that he seemed to fill the room. He was at least six and a half feet tall, seemed almost as wide, in his late thirties. He was in white shirtsleeves, and was wearing a gun in a shoulder harness beneath his left arm.

"I'm Detective Stokes," the man said. "Mr. Adams?"

"That'd be me," Clint said.

"Then you're Temple," Stokes said, "the newspaperman from Boston."

"That's right," Temple said, "or rather, ex-newsman."

"It's my understanding that once you're a newspaperman, you're always a newspaperman. I mean, it's like the ink gets in your blood, right?"

"Pretty much."

Stokes made a point of shaking hands with both of them. His hand was huge.

"Why don't we sit down," Stokes suggested. "We have a lot to go through."

"Sure," Clint said, pulling out a chair. Temple sat across from him.

They sat and discussed the situation for half an hour.

"What you're saying is true, so far," Stokes said to Temple. "He took this girl off a busy street."

"That's the way he works," Temple said. "You'd think he'd want to take them off quiet, deserted streets, but that's not the case."

"He's got a lot of nerve, then," Clint said. "Maybe he's trying to get caught."

"Why would a man want to get caught?" Stokes asked. "What's the point of breaking the law, then?"

"I don't think he wants to be caught," Temple said.

"What do you think, then?" Stokes asked.

"I think he feels there's nobody who can catch him," Temple said. "He's done it enough times now."

"What's the significance of the orange neckerchief?" Stokes asked. "Do you know?"

"I've thought about it a lot," Temple said. "All I can think of is it must be something personal to him."

"So you don't think it's a clue?" the detective asked.

"It might be," Temple said, "but a clue to what? Who he is? Or why he's doing what he's doing?"

"Maybe both," Clint said.

"Where do you think he'll strike next?" Stokes asked.

"I don't know Abilene well," Temple said, "but I'd say you better watch the busy streets, and the young women."

"A lot of streets and even more women in Abilene," Stokes said. "We don't have enough men to cover them all."

"Then you'll just have to do the best you can," Clint said.

"I guess you're right."

"There's one other thing," Temple said.

"What's that?" Stokes asked.

"Somebody took a shot at us last night, out on the street."

"Who?"

"We don't know."

"Was he shooting at both of you?"

"We don't know that either," Clint said.

Stokes sat back in his chair.

"Seems more likely to me that they'd be shooting at you, Mr. Adams."

"That's what I said," Temple commented.

"Well, that's something we'll probably have to find out for ourselves," Clint said. "You've got your own problems."

"I'll have somebody look into it," Stokes said.

"What about witnesses?"

"To the shooting?" Stokes asked.

"To the murder of the girl," Clint said.

"We talked to people on that whole block," Stokes said, "and for another block each way. Nobody saw anything."

"Or they did and they don't know it," Clint said.

"Or they did," Temple agreed, "and they don't know it."

TWELVE

"I don't think we've helped you much, Detective Stokes," Clint said.

"That's not quite true," Stokes said as they all stood up. "Mr. Temple here has given me a little insight into the killer that I didn't have before."

"I hope it helps," Temple said.

"I'll let you know," Stokes said. "I'll have a man walk you out."

"I think we can find the way," Clint said.

"All right." Stokes shook their hands. "If I need anything, where will you be?"

"The Oak Tree Hotel," Clint said. "We each have a room."

"Likewise if you fellas think of anything else, you'll find me right here, unless I'm out on the street. Then you can leave me a message."

"We'll do it, Detective," Clint said.

"Oh, Mr. Adams," Stokes said, "the chief would like to see you in his office before you go."

"We'll stop in there. Just tell us where it is."

"Not him," Stokes said, "just you. He was real specific about that."

Clint looked at Temple.

"I can find my way out," the ex-reporter said. "I'll wait for you out front."

Clint looked at Stokes.

"Okay, then, lead the way."

Stokes took Clint to a large office where Chief Landry was sitting behind a big desk. Behind him the window looked out over the main street.

"Here's Mr. Adams, Chief," he said.

"You finished with him and Temple?" the chief asked without looking up from the papers he was perusing.

"I am for now."

"Okay, then," the chief said. When Stokes didn't move, the chief raised his eyes. "That's all, Stokes."

"Yes, sir."

Stokes withdrew.

"Have a seat Mr. Adams," Landry said. "I wanted to talk to you alone, without your friend Temple, and without the politicians."

"I don't much like politicians myself," Clint said, sitting down.

"Then we have that much in common."

From their earlier meeting, Clint couldn't think of anything else they had in common.

"So why did you want to speak in private?"

"I'm not in favor of this partnership," Landry said, "and by that, I mean my department working with you and Mr. Temple—but the fact is, you are a legend."

He stopped there, when Clint thought there would be more.

"Chief," he said, "is this some kind of . . . apology?"

"I think we got off on the wrong foot," the man said. "Actually, I kinda put my foot in my mouth. I'm just . . . real anxious to catch this killer."

"I don't blame you for that."

"Good," Landry said. "But I have to tell you, I don't like that kid."

"Temple?"

"Yeah, him."

"Well, I've got to tell you, I do. He's given up a lot to go after this killer."

"Yes, after he helped him get out of Boston and basically put him on this trail."

"He made a bad decision in Boston," Clint said. "He's trying to make up for it."

"I just don't want him making any bad decisions here."

"I'm sure he's going to do his best not to."

"I'd appreciate if you kept a tight rein on him."

"Look," Clint said, "he's not writing for any newspaper."

"Good," Landry said, "let's see if we can keep it that way. Did you two get along with Stokes?"

"We did," Clint said. "He seems like a good man."

"He is. In fact, he's my best man," Landry said. "You and he should work real well together."

Clint stood up.

"We'll do our best to help him," he promised.

"That's all I can ask. Thank you for coming to see me."

Clint nodded, left the office, and made his way to the front of the building. Temple was waiting outside.

"What was that all about?"

"Believe it or not," Clint said, "he apologized . . . sort of."

"To you . . . or to us?"

"To me basically," Clint said. "He doesn't like you."

"Can't say I blame him."

"Listen," Clint said, "you're trying to make a difference now. That's all that matters."

"I hope so."

After Clint Adams left his office, Chief Landry sent for Detective Stokes.

"Have a seat, Detective."

"Yes, sir."

"Tell me about your meeting with Adams and Temple."

"Yes, sir." Stokes relayed the meeting as word for word as he could to his boss. Landry listened without saying anything, then remained silent for a few more moments when the man was done. Stokes waited patiently. Patience was a big part of his game.

"All right," Landry said, "I want to have someone watching them at all times."

"I think we got everything from them that they know, sir," Stokes said.

"That may be so, Detective," Landry said, "but that doesn't mean they won't learn more from here on out. Understand?"

"Yes, sir."

"And I want you to use only your best men," the chief said. "I do not want them to know they are being watched."

"Yes, sir."

"See to it."

Stokes nodded, stood up, and left the office.

Landry turned his chair so he could look out the window.

As Temple left the building, he wondered what was on the chief's mind. Was he just trying to separate them? Making Clint some kind of offer? In the short time that he had known Clint Adams, he had come to trust him. If Chief Landry thought he was going to say something to change that, he was going to be disappointed.

Temple didn't like or trust the man, and he figured Clint felt the same way.

The killer, once known as "Mulligan," recognized Harry Temple as soon as he saw him. He didn't know the other man, but he found out soon enough who he was.

He watched as Temple left the building alone and stopped right outside. He watched him, but Temple just stood there, probably waiting for Adams to come out. The best course of action would probably have been to kill him, but that was hard to do in front of the police department building.

Killing Harry Temple would have to wait until another time.

THIRTEEN

Detective Stokes chose two men for the job, Police Officers Benson and Dillon. Both were young—late twenties for Benson, early thirties for Dillon—but good at their jobs.

Temple and Clint Adams were still in front of the building, and he pointed them out.

"Follow those two," he instructed. "I want to know everything they do, everywhere they go, and everyone they talk to."

"Yes, sir," Dillon said.

"The older one is Clint Adams. Do you know that name?"

"The Gunsmith, sir," Benson said.

"Right. Be especially careful with him. He won't be easy to follow without being seen."

"With all due respect, sir," Dillon said, "we're not out on the prairie right now."

"Besides, sir," Benson said, "isn't he a little past his prime?"

Maybe, Stokes thought, he'd chosen the wrong two men.

"If you go into this with that attitude," Stokes said, "he might just hand you your heads. Understand?"

"Yes, sir," Benson said. Dillon nodded.

"Report back to me at the end of each day," he instructed. "Dismissed."

Clint and Temple stopped in the nearest saloon, a small, empty place across the street from the police department. Clint figured it was that nearness to the police that kept the customers away. That, and the early hour.

"A little early for beer, isn't it?" Temple asked as they entered.

"I thought newspapermen drank hard."

"Some do."

"Well," Clint said, "it's never too early for beer. It's the perfect breakfast."

They stopped at the bar and ordered a beer each. The bartender served them up, made no comment on the early hour, and went back to preparing his place for the day.

"So what do you want to do now?" Clint asked.

"What do you mean?"

"You gave the detective what you had," Clint said. "He's going to go out and do his job. What are you going to do?"

"I thought maybe you'd have some ideas."

"This is your game," Clint said. "You're dealing, I'm just playing."

"Dealer's choice, huh?"

"That's right."

Temple played with his beer mug for a few moments.

"I'm not sure," he finally admitted.

"Let me ask you something," Clint said. "Do you think this killer will remember you?"

"Remember me?"

"Yes," Clint said, "by name. Will he remember you as the one who wrote the story that warned him?"

"I don't know," Temple said. "Probably."

"Didn't you say the editor of the paper here offered you a job?"

"Yes . . . so?"

They had both been leaning with their elbows on the bar. Now Clint turned to face Temple.

"I think you should take it."

"What?"

"Take the job."

"But . . . wha—you want him to know I'm here?"

"Sure, why not?"

"But . . . he won't think that's a coincidence. He can't think that."

"What do you think he'll do?" Clint asked. "Run? Or come after you?"

Temple thought a moment, and then his eyes widened.

"You want me to be bait?"

"You said you wanted to catch him."

"Yes, but—"

"You'll have me watching your back the whole time."

"What if seeing my name in the newspaper makes him run again?"

Clint shrugged. "Seems to me that's a chance worth taking."

"What about the police?"

"What about them?"

"Do we tell them what we're planning?"

"No," Clint said. "They wouldn't like it at all."

"B-But . . . I told them I wasn't taking the job."

Clint shrugged again.

"Everybody's entitled to change their mind sometime, aren't they?"

Temple gave it some more thought, then picked up his beer mug.

"I don't know, Clint."

"Well," Clint said, waving to the bartender for two more, "give it some thought. If you can come up with some other plan, I'm all for it."

FOURTEEN

But he didn't.

Temple could not think of any other way to go, so in the end he said, "Yeah, okay. I'll do it."

Clint accompanied him to the newspaper office to talk to the editor.

"What changed your mind?" Pete Tanner asked.

"I'm going to be here a little longer than I thought," Temple said. "I'll need money to live."

"Do his reasons really matter?" Clint asked.

"No, not really," Tanner said. "I'm happy to have a man of his experience on board." He looked at Temple. "Okay, you're hired."

"Thanks."

"And you?" Tanner asked, looking at Clint.

"I'm not looking for a job, thanks," Clint said. "Besides, I'm not a reporter."

"How about an interview?"

"I don't do interviews."

"Not even for a friend?" Tanner asked, indicating Temple.

"Never," Clint said.

"I hope it's not my first assignment to convince him," Temple said.

"No," Tanner said. "Your first assignment is to write whatever you want."

"I'd like to write about the murder of that girl," Temple said, "and why the police have not solved it yet."

"That won't make you any friends with the law," Tanner told him.

"If I was worried about making friends with the law, I never would have written anything wherever I worked," Temple said.

Clint wondered, if Temple had worried about that, would he not be here right now, hunting for a killer? Would the killer not be here, but rather in a prison back East, or even dead?

"I'll leave you to it," Clint said.

Temple turned to face him.

"You said you'd watch my back."

"And I will," Clint said, "but he doesn't even know you're here yet. Not until your first article comes out."

"Maybe."

"Don't worry," Clint said. "I'll be back."

"Where are you going?"

"Just to talk to some people."

"Come," Tanner said, "I'll show you where you can work."

Clint watched as the editor and Temple went farther into the building, then he turned and left.

As Clint Adams left the newspaper office, the two policemen, Dillon and Benson, got into an argument.

Dillon said since he was older, he'd take the Gunsmith, and Benson could stay and watch the newspaperman.

On the other hand, Benson said since he had been with the police department longer, he should follow the Gunsmith, and Dillon should stay with the newspaperman.

In the end they almost lost Clint, but after a quick flip of a coin, Benson took off after him while a morose Dillon stayed to watch out for Temple.

Clint hadn't told Temple, but he had another friend in Abilene, not only Abe Corman. He walked down Main Street and stopped in front of a dress shop called Mathilda's. He looked in the window, saw that there were no customers inside. He opened the door and entered.

He was on his way to interview the local sheriff, whom he'd met briefly when he first came to Abilene. It was his policy to check in with the local law whenever he arrived in a new place, and it was his experience that Western towns that had adopted Eastern police methods and departments usually had a resentful sheriff. That lawman often had information about the police, and the town politicians, that he didn't mind sharing. Information that was not particularly complimentary. This was the kind of information Clint wanted. But since he had to pass the dress shop first—and there were no customers—he decided to stop in.

"Well," the girl behind the counter said, "you don't look like my usual customer."

"You do sell dresses here, don't you?" he asked.

"We do."

She was tall, full-breasted, her face dominated by high cheekbones and huge eyes. When she smiled, she was transformed from pretty into a full beauty. If she had been a saloon girl, men would be fighting over her every night. In fact, Clint would have liked to see her in a low-cut gown, with some makeup on her face. He knew saloon girls who would have killed for her face and figure.

He could stop in to see the sheriff a bit later. After all, he'd already met the man and knew that, more than likely, he'd find him in his office no matter when he went there.

"But I doubt that you're looking for a dress," she said, putting her hands on her hips.

"Why do you say that?"

"Because a man like you would have no need for a dress," she said.

"What if I had a wife?"

She laughed. "A man like you has no need for a wife!"

"You seem pretty sure of yourself," he said, approaching the counter.

"I'm very sure."

"You're very confident."

She raised her chin. "Shouldn't I be?"

"Maybe not."

He reached over the counter to grab her and pull her across. He gathered her into his arms and kissed her. Her mouth became soft and pliant beneath his.

"Clint," she said, gasping, "one of my customers could come walking in here any minute."

"Then maybe I should lock the door," he said with his mouth against her neck. The smell of her was intoxicating.

He kissed her again, and this time her mouth was aggressive rather than compliant. When they broke, they were both breathless from it.

"To hell with the door," she gasped. "Just take me into the back room and fuck me!"

FIFTEEN

He half dragged, half carried her into the back storage room.

She was wearing a simple cotton dress, so when they got into the back room, he simply tore it off her—after all, she had plenty of dresses there to replace it with.

When he had her naked, he carried her to a pile of cloth bolts and laid her down on them.

"Hey!" she protested. "You know my customers are going to want to make dresses from this cloth."

"And they'll be very special dresses," he told her.

She laughed and watched, languishing naked on the bed of cloth, while he removed his gun belt, set it aside within easy reach, and then took off the rest of his clothes. She always caught her breath when his erect penis—the most beautiful she had ever seen—came into view.

"Come here," she said, reaching out to grasp him by the cock and pull him to her.

He climbed on top of her and began to kiss her face, her neck, her shoulders. She shivered as he worked his way lower. He had to slide off the cloth bolt bed in order to get down between her legs. She lifted them for him, spread them, and curled her toes as his tongue went to work on her.

"Oh God," she called out, "I hope nobody comes in . . . maybe we should have locked the door . . . oh, do that, yeah . . . do that some more . . . right there . . ."

She was very aggressive in her lovemaking, which Clint liked, but she also had a habit of talking during sex. This may have only been the third time they were together, but this was clearly the trend.

"Oh, yes!"

In the offices of the *Abilene Reporter-News*, Temple was sitting at a typewriter for the first time in months. And for the first time in two years he was writing about Mulligan— or whatever the killer was calling himself these days.

"How's it coming?" Tanner asked from behind him.

Temple turned, looked at his new editor standing in the doorway of his shoebox office.

"I am getting comfortable with it again."

"The typewriter?"

"Writing."

"May I?"

"Have a look? Sure."

Tanner came up to the desk and read over Temple's shoulder.

"Well," he said, "I can see you haven't lost your touch. Just from what I see here, I think the chief of police is not going to be very happy with you."

"I didn't think my job was to keep the chief happy," Temple said.

"It's not."

"You're not afraid of him coming after your newspaper?" Temple asked.

"I wish he would," Tanner said. "It would be great publicity."

"So I should keep going."

"You should definitely keep going."

"Keep going!" Mattie yelled. "Keep going!"

Clint had climbed back on top of Mathilda on the cloth bed and driven his raging cock into her. She wrapped her legs around his waist, and as he pummeled her, she began to shout, "Keep going!" As if he were planning to stop. In fact, he couldn't have stopped if a gaggle of women had just entered the dress shop.

Then they heard the bell over the front door tinkle.

SIXTEEN

"Ladies!" Mathilda said, coming out of the back room, smoothing her hair down, trying to control her breathing. "How nice to see you."

The three middle-aged women turned and smiled at her.

"We didn't think you were here, Mathilda," one of them said.

"I was just . . . in the back room, doing some work."

"Are you all right, my dear?" one of the others asked. "You look . . . flushed."

Mattie put her hand to her breast and said, "I was just . . . moving some heavy boxes."

"You need a man around here to do that for you, my girl," the third woman said.

"And for other things," the first one said, and the three of them tittered.

"You're right, of course," she said. "I do need a man around here." She moved around behind the counter and asked. "What can I get for you ladies?"

Clint barely had his pants on when he snuck out the back door. He strapped on his gun belt and walked down the alley on rubbery legs. When he reached the street, he headed in the direction of the sheriff's office. He resisted the urge to look in the window of the dress shop again.

Clint knocked on the door of the sheriff's office and entered. The lawman was seated behind his desk, seemingly in the same position he was when Clint checked in with him the first day he came to town.

"Adams," the lawman said. "I heard you were havin' yourself a good time playin' poker. Must be true, since you're still here."

"Do you ever leave your office, Sheriff?"

Sheriff Milt Evans laughed shortly, but with no humor, and said, "What for? They've got their new police department. What do they need me for?"

"Well," Clint said, "I need you to answer a few questions. Mind if I sit?"

"Be my guest. Drink?" There was a bottle and a coffee cup on the desk. The older man's hand shook as he reached for the bottle. His scalp gleamed pink through what was left of his white hair.

"No, thanks."

Evans arrested his movement and left the bottle where it was.

"Okay, then," he said, "what can I do for you?"

"Seems to me if anyone can tell me about the chief of police, it's you," Clint said.

"And why is that?"

"Because the town hiring him has turned you into . . . well, this."

Evans sat back in his chair.

"You know, that doesn't insult me."

"I wasn't trying to insult you."

"Chief Landry . . . are you involved with him?"

"I am," Clint said. "A friend of mine and I are working on the murder of Laurie Wilson with him."

"Oh, that."

"What do you know about that?"

"I know I tried to get involved and was invited to stay out of it."

"By who? The chief?"

"And the mayor."

"I see."

"So yeah, if you want some information on our chief, and our mayor, I'm your man. And if you're gonna catch that killer, I want to be part of it."

Clint looked at the whiskey bottle on the desk. Evans saw where his eyes went, took the bottle off the desk, and put it in a drawer.

"Okay then," Clint said, "fill me in."

When Clint left the sheriff's office a half hour later, he knew more about Chief Landry and Mayor Stanley then he ever thought he would. He also knew more about the district attorney, Ned Beaumont. All he had to do now was relay the information to Temple.

They also had another ally in Sheriff Evans, maybe an ally they could trust more than Chief Landry. He still wasn't sure about Detective Stokes. Evans wasn't able to help much with him. He didn't know the man.

Clint returned the way he had come, bypassed the dress shop, and made his way back to the newspaper office.

SEVENTEEN

When he walked in, he found the place quiet. The printing press was lying dormant for the moment. Somewhere from the back, though, he could hear a typewriter, and he followed the sound.

First he came to Tanner's office. The man swiveled around in his chair.

"He's farther back," he told Clint. "Just follow the sound down the hall."

He did that and came to a room no bigger than a closet. Harry Temple was sitting at a typewriter, oblivious to anything but the paper he was writing on.

"Looks like you got right back into it," Clint said.

Temple swiveled around on a creaky chair and smiled, holding his hands and wriggling his fingers.

"Like I never left," he said.

"You almost done with that?" Clint asked.

"Close. You got news?"

"I've got information," Clint said. "Thought we'd go get some coffee and talk about it."

"Coffee?" Temple asked. "Not beer?"

Clint looked at him as if he was crazy and said, "A little early for beer, isn't it?"

* * *

Temple finished his story while Clint waited, then they went down the hall together and he handed it to Tanner.

"Do whatever you think needs to be done to it," he said. "I may be a bit rusty."

"I'm sure it's fine," Tanner said. "It'll be in tomorrow's early edition."

"I'll be back," Temple said. "We can talk about what else I can do around here."

"Good enough," Tanner said.

He was already back at work as they went out the front door.

Abilene was big enough to have several of everything—saloons, hotels, restaurants, and cafés. Clint found a café he hadn't been to yet, and they went in and got a table. They ordered coffee and pie from a bored waiter. Either the place didn't do a lively business, or they were waiting for the next rush.

"What have you got?" Temple asked.

"I had a talk with the sheriff," Clint said. "He's not a big supporter of the local police, or administration."

"I thought you didn't have much use for him," Temple said. It was one of the things they'd discussed over a beer.

"I didn't, but I've changed my mind. He's just upset about being edged out as the main law in town, so he did his research into his replacements."

"And?"

"He doesn't know much about Stokes, but apparently Chief Landry had been fired from his last three jobs—one back East, and two as he moved west."

"Why?"

"The most Sheriff Evans could find out was something about incompetence."

"He strike you as incompetent?"

"No," Clint said.

"But if that's his reputation, why would he be hired?" Temple asked.

"Again, according to the sheriff, Landry and Mayor Stanley are old friends."

"Ahh . . ."

"As for Mayor Stanley," Clint went on, "he's a frustrated politician who likely won't move much further in his career than he is now."

"And Beaumont?"

"Evans doesn't know much about the district attorney," Clint said. "Just that he's a lawyer Stanley moved into the position after the previous district attorney died."

"Died?"

"Natural causes."

"So no foul play there."

"No."

"Hmm."

"What are you thinking?"

"Well, since I'm going to be here," Temple said, "maybe I should do a story on the present administration. You think the sheriff would talk to me?"

"I don't see why not."

"On the record?"

"That you'd have to ask him."

Temple considered that for a moment, making circles on the table with his coffee cup.

"Maybe I will," he said thoughtfully.

"You know, you really don't have to do anything else," Clint said. "That story of yours will either do the job tomorrow, or it won't."

"Well," Temple said with a shrug, "like I said, since I'm here."

EIGHTEEN

Temple decided to go and talk to the sheriff right away. Clint went with him to watch his back on the street, but remained outside while Temple went in.

Clint wasn't sure why Temple wanted to attack the Abilene mayor and the chief of police. He was going to have enough trouble when his article about the murder came out the next day.

On the one hand, it could make the killer go after him. But on the other, it could have the same effect his article in Boston had, and make the killer run.

There was a difference this time, though. Temple was ready if the killer ran—this time he had Clint to help him track him properly.

But there was another possibility, and that was that the killer was already gone, having been satisfied with the one murder.

There was a chair outside the sheriff's office, which Clint put to good use. After about a half hour, Harry Temple came back out, tucking some notes into his shirt pocket.

Clint stood and asked, "Get anything good?"

"Abilene," Temple said, "may turn out to be fun."

* * *

Temple decided to return to the newspaper office and work on his next story. Clint walked him back to the front door, and stopped there.

"I'll be safe here," Temple said.

"Yeah, you will," Clint said, "especially since you've got a policeman watching you. We both do."

"What? Where?"

"Don't look around," Clint said. "Act natural. Right now they're both across the street, but when you go inside and I walk away, one of them will follow me."

"How long have they been there?"

"Since we left the police building."

"So the chief . . ."

Clint nodded. "He's having us followed."

"Followed, or guarded?" Temple asked.

"Might be the same thing," Clint said. "When you come back to the hotel, don't look around. Don't let him know you know he's there."

"I won't."

"If I can," Clint said, "I'll walk you back myself."

"I have a gun."

"Yeah, I've been meaning to ask you about that," Clint said. "Can you shoot that thing?"

"All you've got to do is pull the trigger, right?"

"Have you ever done it?"

"Sure."

"To shoot at what?"

"Bottle, cans . . . trees."

"A man?"

Temple hesitated, then said, "N-No, I've never shot at a man."

"When we get back to the hotel tonight, let me have a look at it."

"I keep it clean."

"I'll have a look anyway," Clint said, then added, "if you don't mind."

"Well . . . all right," Temple said. "After all, you are the gun man."

"Yes," Clint said, "yes, I am. I'm . . . the gun . . . man."

Temple nodded and went inside. When he closed the door, Clint could see by the reflection in the window that the two policemen were still across the street.

He turned and walked toward the hotel.

NINETEEN

"This time," Dillon said to Benson, "I want Adams."

"Be my guest," Benson said. "He didn't do nothing before anyway. I'd just as soon sit here and relax."

Dillon frowned, as if he had made the wrong decision, then started after Clint.

Clint walked slowly to the hotel, aware that one of the policemen was following him, staying to the other side of the street while he did it. The two men were young, and probably thought Clint couldn't see them because they were in town, and not out on the trail.

He considered stopping at the dress shop again, but knew Mathilda would not be so cavalier about having sex this time—not after almost getting caught. But hey, it was her idea not to lock the door.

He kept walking and stopped only when he got to the Big Horn Saloon. He went inside and right to the bar, using the mirror behind it to see if the policeman followed him in. He didn't.

"Beer?" the bartender asked. After three days the man knew what Clint wanted.

"Yeah."

The saloon was quiet. It was still too early for the gambling to have started, or for the girls to have come down. There was only one girl working the place at the moment.

"Gonna take some more money off the mayor?" the bartender asked, leaning on the bar.

"Sure, if he's willing," Clint said.

"I hope you do," the man said.

"Why?"

"That blowhard deserves it."

"You don't like the mayor?"

"Nobody does."

"Then why is he the mayor?"

"Because nobody ever runs against him, that's why."

"Why not?"

"Well, for one thing, nobody wants the job," the bartender said. "And for another, nobody wants to go against him."

"What about Beaumont?"

"He's the mayor's right hand, not as bad, but still a bastard."

"I see. So if somebody did come out against them, the town would support him?"

"Well now," the bartender said, "that would depend on who it was. You interested in either job?"

"Not me," Clint said. "But there might be somebody in town who would be."

"Like who?"

"You own this place?"

"Sure do."

The man was in his forties, old enough to have been around some.

"Why don't you run?"

He laughed. "Mister, I know how to run a saloon," he said, shaking his head, "not a town."

"So you can't think of anyone in this town who should run?" Clint asked.

"Should? Yeah, a few," the barman said. "But would they?

Naw. 'Scuse me." Another customer came in and he moved down the bar to serve him.

Clint picked up his beer, looked up at the big horns above the mirror that the saloon was named after. He turned then to look over the interior of the room as he sipped his beer. There were a few faces he knew were regulars, but no one he had ever really exchanged words with before.

He still had most of the day in front of him. He just didn't know what to do with it.

TWENTY

Clint had ordered a second beer and taken it to a table when the batwings swung inward and Sheriff Evans walked in. He stopped, spotted Clint, then went to the bar for a beer and carried it over.

"Mind if I join you?"

"Sure, have a seat."

The sheriff pulled out a chair and sat across from Clint, not blocking Clint's view of the room and the front door.

"I had an interesting talk with your young partner," Evans said.

"I heard."

"Looks like he's decided to take on the town fathers."

"From what I've heard, somebody should," Clint said.

"You gonna back his play?"

"Which one?" Clint asked. "Against the killer, or against the town fathers?"

"Well . . . both."

"Sure, why not."

"You played poker with the mayor and Ned Beaumont," Evans said.

"That doesn't mean we're friends," Clint said. "In fact, I learned more about them in a few minutes talking to you than I did the whole time I was playing poker with them. All I learned then was that they were bad poker players."

"And now?"

"It seems as if they're not what you'd call unselfish civil servants."

Evans laughed and said, "You've got them pegged!"

"Seems to me this town needs some new blood in office," Clint said.

"Sure does," Evans said, "but there ain't nobody who'll give it a try."

"What about you?"

Evans almost choked on his beer, slammed the mug down on the table hard enough to spill some of it.

"What?"

"Why don't you run for mayor?"

"I ain't no politician."

"Seems to me that makes you perfect for the job," Clint said. "And why do I have a feeling you're not afraid of Mayor Stanley?"

"That jasper?" Evans made a rude sound with his mouth, then picked up his beer and took a healthy swig, as if he was trying to wash a bad taste from his mouth. "There's lots of things I'm afraid of, but he ain't one of them."

"Then maybe you should run."

"You know," Evans said, "ain't nobody gonna run against him unless they see a chink in his armor."

"Well," Clint said, "maybe you'll see one soon."

Evans cocked his head. "The kid? Is he gonna write somethin'?"

"You'll have to wait and see."

Evans leaned on the table and looked Clint directly in the eye.

"If your boy can write something that exposes Mayor Stanley . . ."

"You'll run?"

"I ain't as old as I look, you know," Evans said. "It's the white hair. Maybe it is time for a career change."

"I'll drink to that," Clint said, picking up his beer. He sipped it and set it down. "Don't look for it in tomorrow's edition, because there's going to be something else . . . but it's coming."

"I'll watch for it," Evans said. He finished his beer and stood up. "Guess I better go and do my rounds, let people see I'm still here."

TWENTY-ONE

Walking back to the newspaper office later in the day, Clint was tempted to confront the policeman who was following him, but he decided against it. Let Chief Landry think he had succeeded in putting an unseen tail on him.

When he reached the door of the *Reporter-News*, it was locked. He tried to see inside, but it looked dark. He framed his face against the glass and thought he saw a light farther in. He knocked on the door, then knocked again. Finally he saw someone coming toward it.

When the door opened, it was Harry Temple.

"What happened?" Clint asked.

"Nothing," Temple said. "Tanner went home, closed up the shop. He told me when I was done, I could go out the back door. Come on in."

Clint entered and they locked the front door behind them. Temple led the way back to his closet-sized office. Clint could see sheets of paper next to the typewriter, and one in the machine that Temple was working on.

"Is that about Mayor Stanley?"

"Yeah," Temple said, "mostly some stuff that Evans told me. You want to read it?"

"Whatever it says," Clint replied, "could I talk you out of it?"

"No," Temple said. "This will be the first time I've had my say in two years."

"You don't know much about Abilene politics, though."

"I know a blowhard when I see one," Temple said, "and so far since I've been here, I've seen two."

"But all you have to go on is what Evans gave you."

"Sheriff Evans is believable."

"Even though he has an ax to grind?"

"Often," Temple said, "in my business, those are the people who are the most believable."

"If you say so. Are you done here?"

"Sure, why not?" Temple said. "I can finish this tomorrow."

"Tomorrow your strangler piece comes out," Clint said. "Starting in the morning, you'll have a target on your back."

"Then let's go and get something to eat tonight," Temple said, "while we can dine in peace."

"Well, that sounds like the Cattleman's Palace," Clint said.

"Sounds like the perfect place for a hearty last meal," Temple said. He started for the back door, but Clint stopped him.

"If we go out the back, the two policemen will lose us."

"Tanner left me a key," Temple said. "We can go out the front and lock the door behind us."

"Let's do that."

Temple shrugged and they walked to the front door.

They walked slowly so there would be no chance the two policemen would lose them.

Now that Temple knew they were there, he said, "They might as well be in uniform. They're not very good at this."

"I know," Clint said. "Makes me wonder why they were even given the job."

"What are you thinking?"

"They weren't assigned by the chief," Clint said.

"Stokes?"

"That's what I'm thinking."

"Why?"

"Because the chief told him to assign two men," Clint said. "Probably his best men."

"And Stokes assigned these two," Temple said. "He wanted you to see them."

"Yeah," Clint said. "Like a warning."

"Again: Why?"

"We'll have to find that out," Clint said, "won't we?"

TWENTY-TWO

At the Cattleman's Palace they were seated immediately at a table that suited Clint. He could see the entire room, and there was nobody behind him.

A waiter came and took their orders for steak dinners with all the trimmings. He returned, bringing them each a cold mug of beer.

"Maybe we should send some food across the street to those two policemen."

"That would send them running back to Stokes," Clint said. "It would be funny, but first I want to find out what's on Stokes's mind."

"How are you going to do that?"

"It's simple," Clint said. "I'm going to ask him."

"When?"

"Tomorrow."

"I'll be interested in his answer."

They sat back and allowed the waiter to set down their huge platters of meat and vegetables, which suspended all conversation while they ate.

Across the street the policemen, Dillon and Benson, stood in a doorway and grumbled.

"They're havin' a great meal and we have to stand out here and starve," Dillon said.

"We're doing our jobs," Benson said. "Stop grumbling." But he was no happier than the younger man about being stuck out there, across the street from all that food, starving.

"Why don't you go and get somethin' to eat?" Dillon complained.

"And what if they come out while I'm doin' that?" Benson asked. "No, sir, I ain't gettin' bawled out by Stokes because I was off gettin' you somethin' to eat. So just shut up and watch."

"You shut up," Dillon grumbled.

The killer watched the two policemen bicker from his position across the street and down the block from the Palace. He knew that the Eastern newspaperman was inside, along with Clint Adams.

He knew that killing Harry Temple would be both easy and a pleasure, but the Gunsmith, that would be another matter. That would be . . . exciting. He could have left town and moved on, but the challenges here had become too great.

And it seemed like a long time since he'd strangled that girl. He needed another kill.

Mayor Theodore Stanley looked up as his office door opened and Chief Landry came in.

"Chief," he said. "Have a seat."

Landry sat down without a word.

"Who do you have working on this murder?"

"Detective Stokes."

"Is he a good man?"

"He's the best I've got, Mayor."

"Did you put him together with Adams and that newspaperman?"

"I did," Landry said. "They had a conversation."

"So where do we stand?"

"Strokes has two men watching them."

"And?"

"And he's using what the newspaperman told him to try and find this killer."

"You've had plenty of time to find this man," the mayor said. "I'm getting tired of waiting."

"Well," Landry said, "police work is usually a lot of waiting."

"I'm not pleased with that answer, Chief."

"We're doing the best we can, Mayor."

The mayor leaned forward in his chair and said, "Do better!"

After the chief left, the door opened again and Ned Beaumont came in.

"Well?" he asked.

"I don't know," the mayor said. "Landry assigned a man named Stokes, and he's spoken to Adams and Temple, but I don't know."

"What else is there to do?" Beaumont asked. "Can you think of anybody else to bring in?"

"No," Stanley said, "but I have an election later this year. If we don't catch that killer, I'm not going to have my job much longer."

"Seems to me we've got plenty of people working on this now," Beaumont said. "The kid, Temple, is the key, I think. He's dealt with the killer before."

"I don't much care who catches him," Mayor Stanley said, "I just want him caught!"

TWENTY-THREE

After dinner, Clint and Temple walked back to their hotel. Clint kept himself very alert. The article may not have come out yet, but they had already been shot at once. Whichever of them was the intended target, it could happen again.

If it did happen this time, there'd be two policemen right behind them who might see something.

So Clint had to remain alert without letting the two policemen know that he was aware of their presence.

"You know that target you said would be on my back?" Temple asked.

"Yes."

"I already feel it."

"I know what you mean," Clint said. "I feel one on my back, too."

"Well," Temple said, "at least I'm not alone."

They got to the front door of their hotel without being shot at. Clint stopped just inside the lobby.

"What is it?"

"I'm just wondering if those two are going to stay outside all night."

"Wouldn't be a bad idea if they did," Temple observed. "Would it?"

"Maybe one will stay and the other will go and report our movements," Clint said. He slapped the younger man on the back. "Get some rest. Tomorrow could be a big day. And it could be just the beginning."

"I just hope he's not already gone," Temple said, "because then it's all for nothing."

They went up the stairs together, each to his own room.

"Okay," Benson said, "you stay here and I'll go report in to the boss."

"Why do I have to stay?" Dillon demanded. "You stay and I'll go talk to Stokes."

"Stop arguin' with me—"

"Then stop tryin' to be in charge all the time."

"Look," Benson said, "they're in their rooms. They're not goin' anywhere. Let's go get somethin' to eat, and then we'll both report to Stokes."

"Okay," Dillon said, "okay, yeah. That works for me."

They started walking down the street.

"So," Dillon said, "where do you wanna eat . . ."

The killer watched Clint Adams and Harry Temple enter the hotel, then watched the two policemen argue before they walked away.

He moved from the hotel side of the street to the other side, so he could clearly see the entire building. He could have sneaked into the hotel and taken care of Temple tonight, but he was interested in seeing what Temple had been doing at the newspaper office. So he was going to put Temple's death off a day or two. Then once he was taken care of, that would leave the Gunsmith.

He watched the hotel for about a half an hour, just for want of something else to do, before turning and walking off into the darkness.

* * *

When Clint got to his room, he looked out his window at
the street below. He thought he saw someone in the darkness across the street, but the longer he stared, the harder it
became to make anything out. He finally gave up and
moved away from the window.

He took a straight-backed wooden chair from the corner and jammed it under the doorknob. There was no way
for anyone to get in the window, so with that done, he
removed his boots and his gun belt, hanging the latter on
the bedpost. He then settled down on the bed with a book,
which he hoped would occupy his mind until he got sleepy.

In his room, Harry Temple sat on his bed and wondered
about some of his recent decisions. Discovering that Clint
Adams was in Abilene and then recruiting him still seemed
logical to him. He'd been chasing this killer for two years
alone. Now he finally had an ally. But Clint's idea to dan-
gle Temple as bait, that he wasn't so sure about. Well, it
was done now. The piece would come out in the morning
paper, and that was that. But that didn't mean he was going
to be able to sleep.

Or maybe this would be his last chance to get a good
night's sleep. After tonight, like Clint had said, there'd be a
target on his back.

He got undressed, slid under the sheet, and tried to
sleep.

Clint was reading Dickens when there was a light knock
on the door. He wondered if it was Temple. Maybe the
young man was unable to sleep. He wouldn't have blamed
him. Not at all.

He got up from the bed, put down the book, took his
gun from his holster, and walked to the door.

TWENTY-FOUR

"Who's there?"

"Who do you think?" a woman's voice asked. "How many women do you know in town who would come to your door?"

"Mattie?"

"Of course," she said. "Let me in before somebody sees me standing in the hall."

He moved the chair, unlocked the door, and opened it. She slipped in.

"Quick," she said, "close the door."

He did so, then turned to face her.

"Are you gonna shoot me?"

He looked down at the gun in his hand, forgotten for the moment.

"Of course not."

He walked to the bed and put it back in the holster, then turned to her again.

"Mattie, what are you doing here?"

"We started something this morning that we didn't finished," she said.

"You shouldn't be here."

"I've been here before."

"That was different."

"How?"

"There was no danger before."

"And there is now?"

"Yes, possibly."

"From what?"

"A man."

She sat down on the bed. She was wearing a cotton dress and a sweater she said she had knitted herself.

"You're being cryptic," she said. "Tell me what's going on."

He sat on the bed next to her.

"Okay," he said, "you know about the girl who was strangled."

"Laurie."

"You knew her?"

"She was a customer. I was so sorry when she was killed. What about her?"

"I'm helping to find her killer."

"But that's wonderful. Are you doing it alone?"

"No, not alone."

"Who are you working with?"

"Well, the police."

"And?"

"What do you mean, 'and'?"

"I heard an 'and.'"

"I'm working with somebody else," he admitted, "but you don't know him."

"Maybe I'd like to meet him if he's gonna help you find Laurie's killer."

"Okay," he said, "maybe."

"You still haven't told me why it's dangerous to be here with you."

"You know who I am."

"The big bad Gunsmith that everybody's afraid of," she said. "Only you're not so scary to me."

She leaned over and kissed him. The kiss went on for some time, and then he pulled away.

"I should send you packing," he said.

"You think the killer's gonna come after you here?"

"You never know."

"How does he know you're after him?"

"He doesn't, not for sure," he said. "But he will know by tomorrow."

She slid her hand across his stomach and pressed her face close to his. "Then we have until tomorrow."

This time he kissed her . . .

When Abe Corman answered the knock at his door, he found Pete Tanner standing there.

"Hey, Pete," he said. "Didn't hear you ride up."

"Came in my buggy."

"Come on in," Corman said. "Drink?"

"Just a quick one," Tanner said. "I gotta get back. I just wanted to check something with you."

Corman led him into the living room, poured two glasses of brandy, and handed one to the editor.

"What's going on?"

"Clint Adams," Tanner said after a sip. "I understand he's a friend of yours. At least, that's what I heard."

"Yes, he is."

"He and Harry Temple, they're after this man who strangled Laurie Wilson."

"And?"

"Temple's got an article in the paper tomorrow that's really going to heat things up."

"Look, Pete," Corman said, "the strangler is one man, and Clint Adams can handle any one man."

"Are you sure?"

"I'm positive."

"Okay, then." Tanner tossed off the drink. "Got to get back. I need to get the early edition out."

"I'll look forward to reading it."

He walked Tanner to the door, closed it behind him, hoping to God he *was* right.

TWENTY-FIVE

Mattie liked the way Clint's cock felt inside her when she had her legs in the air. And when he grabbed her ankles and spread her even more, she gasped. He drove himself into her, grunting with the effort. She did her best to meet each of his thrusts, and their effort covered them with perspiration. The sweat made her body gleam in the light from the wall lamp. It enflamed his ardor even more, causing his penis to feel even harder. He felt as if he were battering her with a railroad tie.

"Oh God, yes, Clint, yes," she said, keeping up a steady stream of dialogue, some of his the dirtiest talk he'd ever heard. "Fuck me, damnit, fuck me harder, come on, do it, split me . . ."

"Mattie," he grunted, "for once in your life . . . shut up!"

After that she grunted and groaned, and yelled, but tried not to blather on. Finally, she screamed when he exploded inside her, but he could barely hear her because of his own roar . . .

Mattie sat cross-legged on the bed, still naked, with her hands over her mouth.

"I didn't mean to scream," she said. "Do you think anybody heard me?"

"I hardly heard you," he said, "but then I was pretty loud, too."

He was standing at the window, also naked, looking out.

"Anybody out there?" she asked.

"It's dark," he said. "Can't tell."

He turned back toward the interior of the room. Mattie was now sitting with her hands down, and he had a clear view of her full, somewhat chubby breasts. She was tall, and when she was dressed, her breasts didn't seem that big, but when she was naked, he could see the deep undersides in all their glory, as well at the dark nipples and wide areolae.

"God, you're beautiful," he said.

"And sweaty," she said.

"That's part of it."

She stared at his crotch and said, "You're not so bad yourself. Bring that over here."

"I think I still need a few minutes," Clint told her.

"I can get you up for the job," she said confidently.

He looked down at his penis, which was semierect and hardening.

"I seem to be doing all right myself," he pointed out.

"I still want you over here," she said, patting the mattress.

He started for the bed, saying, "Be careful what you wish for."

Harry Temple thought he heard a scream, and then a yell.

He rolled over in bed and listened, but there was nothing further. Unsure about whether or not he'd really heard what he thought he heard, he got up and walked to the door. Pressing his ear to it, he listened, but there was nothing. Maybe he had been dreaming.

He went back to bed, but couldn't sleep. He thought about going down the hall to Clint's room to see if he was asleep, but after all, Clint was the Gunsmith. He probably never had a problem sleeping.

Maybe a drink would help, but he had no whiskey. And leaving the hotel and going to a saloon alone would be taking a chance. He looked over at his gun belt, sitting on the chair where he'd put it. He really wasn't very good with it. He wasn't a fool. If he was going to get through this, he was going to have to depend on Clint Adams's gun.

Clint rolled onto his back and tried to catch his breath.

"I get it now," he said. "You're going to try to kill me before anybody else does."

"I just figure I should take advantage of you while I have you," she said. "Starting tomorrow morning, who knows when I'll get to see you again—if at all."

He didn't comment.

She rolled over and pressed her chin to his shoulder.

"You're not going to get killed, are you, Clint?" she asked.

"Not if I can help it, Mattie."

"Well," she said, "maybe you could help it by not making a target of yourself."

"Actually," Clint said, "it's not me who's the target."

"It's the other fella?" she asked. "The one you're working with?"

"I'm afraid so," Clint said. "And he needs me to watch his back."

"Can't the law watch his back?"

Clint put his arm around her and pulled her close, nuzzled her hair.

"They can watch their own backs."

TWENTY-SIX

Dillon and Benson stood in front of the police department building.

"Nobody's here," Dillon said. "What are we supposed to do now?"

"Stokes said we had to report," Benson said. "So we better report."

"Wait," Dillon said. "You sayin' we should go to his house?"

"That's where he's gonna be, ain't it?"

"Well, yeah, but—"

"What do you think we should do?"

"I don't know—"

"Then let's go," Benson said. "If you think of a better idea on the way, you can let me know."

The door was answered by a handsome-looking woman in her mid-thirties.

"Mrs. Stokes," Benson said. "We're looking for your husband."

She didn't look happy. "Wait here."

She closed the door in their faces. Moments later Stokes opened the door, holding a napkin, and glared at them.

"You men were supposed to report in at the end of the day!" he said.

Benson looked confused.

"We are."

"I meant at headquarters!"

"B-But . . . you said to stay with them 'til the end of the day," Benson said. "They turned in a little while ago."

"So they're at their hotel?"

"Yeah."

"Then what are you doing here?" Stokes asked. "At least one of you should be watching it all night."

"All night?" Dillon asked.

"All night," Stokes said. "Then one of you report to me in the morning. Now get out of here. Don't come to my house again!"

He slammed the door on them.

Dillon looked at Benson and said, "Told you this was a bad idea."

Mattie left in the morning.

"I need a bath before work," she said.

"You smell fine to me," Clint said to her at the door.

"My customers won't think so," she said. "They'll smell you all over me."

"The old biddies who come to your store don't remember the smell of a man on a woman."

"You're forgetting that Laura was a customer in my store," she reminded him. She poked him in the chest with her finger. "Find whoever killed her."

"I intend to."

She kissed him and left.

After cleaning up in the basin in his room, Clint went down to the lobby. Temple was already there, sitting in a chair, waiting.

"When did you get up?" Clint asked.

"Earlier than you."

"Couldn't sleep?"

"Not very well."

"Scared?"

"Yep."

"Good," Clint said, "you should be. Come on. I'll buy you breakfast."

"And the condemned ate a hearty meal," Temple said, following Clint into the dining room.

"Wait a minute," Temple said a little while later. "You knew Mark Twain?"

"I *know* Samuel Clemens," Clint said. "Who happens to use the name 'Mark Twain.'"

"Wow," Temple said, "that man is a brilliant storyteller."

"And writer."

Temple shrugged.

"What? You don't think Mark Twain is a brilliant writer?" Clint asked.

"Don't get me wrong," Temple said, cutting the ham on his plate, "like I said, a brilliant storyteller, but as a writer? I think he needs a good editor."

"Jesus Christ!" Clint said. "What about Dickens?"

"Again," Temple said, "a great storyteller."

"Okay, smart guy," Clint said, "so who's a great writer?"

"Edgar Allan Poe."

"Wasn't he a drunk?"

"What's that got to do with writing?" Temple asked.

"You have a point. Who else?"

"Robert Louis Stevenson. *Treasure Island.* Amazing."

"I met Stevenson."

Temple dropped his fork.

"Just in passing once," Clint said, "on a train."

Temple got over his shock, picked up his fork, and asked, "Who else have you met?"

TWENTY-SEVEN

After breakfast Clint and Temple walked over to the *Reporter-News* office. As they walked in, Pete Tanner slapped copies of the early edition into their hands.

"There you have it!" he exclaimed. "It's already on the street."

"Good," Temple said without enthusiasm.

Clint didn't comment; he just started reading the article. In it, Temple pointed out how the killer had started in Boston, how the police there couldn't catch him, and how since then he'd moved west, each time killing without being caught. Then Temple spent a couple of paragraphs on the Abilene murder, and how lost the Abilene police were. He then assured the public that he knew how this killer worked, and before long—with his help—the man would be caught.

"You didn't put 'Mulligan' in here," Clint commented.

"That hasn't been his name since Boston," Temple pointed out.

"What about a description?"

"I've never seen him," Temple said, "and the descriptions have varied."

"But . . . you said you had information about who he was, and that's why he left Boston."

"Right," Temple said, "I had the name 'Mulligan.' "

Clint lowered the paper and looked at Temple.

"That's it?" he asked. "That's all you had?"

"What did you think I had?"

"I thought you knew who he was," Clint said, "and that was why he left Boston."

"I never said that."

"You never said you didn't."

Tanner smirked and said, "That's newspaperman talk. Never let 'em know what you have, and what you don't have."

"So we really don't know who we're looking for," Clint said.

"No," Temple said, "but thanks to this article, he knows who he's looking for."

"That target on your back just got a whole lot bigger," Clint said.

"Are you saying you can't protect me?" Temple asked.

"No," Clint said, "I'm just saying it'll be harder to watch your back when I don't know who I'm watching for."

"Your other piece is in tomorrow's edition," Tanner said.

"What?" Temple asked, whipping his head around to look at Tanner.

"The one about the mayor and the chief?" Tanner said. "Tomorrow."

"Great," Temple said, "then by tomorrow morning, they'll want me dead, too."

"Sonofabitch!" the chief of police said.

Stokes stood in front of the man's desk, remaining silent.

"Have you seen this?" the chief demanded, waving the newspaper over his head.

"Yes, sir."

"This is how he intends to help catch a killer?" Landry demanded. "By making us seem like we're lost."

"We are kind of lost, sir."

"I don't want to hear that, Detective!" Landry exploded.

"No, sir."

The chief slammed the newspaper down on his desk.

"There is one thing this article accomplishes," Stokes added.

"And what might that be?"

"It puts a target right on this reporter's back," Stokes said. "The killer is bound to make a try at him."

Landry thought a moment, then said, "I suppose you could look at it that way. You still got two men watching them?"

"I do."

"Good men?"

"They could be better," Stokes said after a moment's hesitation.

"Then put somebody better on the job," Landry said. "And do it fast!"

"Yes, sir," Stokes said. "I'll see to it."

As Stokes left the office, the chief sat down and covered his face with both hands. Any moment now he expected to get a message from the mayor, and he wasn't looking forward to it.

"Did you see this?" the mayor asked Ned Beaumont. He was upset, but covered it up a lot better than Chief Landry did.

"I did," Beaumont said.

"This young fella is looking to get himself killed."

"I think he's depending on the Gunsmith to keep that from happening, Mayor."

"Well, he better hope he's putting his trust in the right man," Mayor Stanley said.

"Yes, sir."

"Get word to the chief that I want to see him," the mayor said. "Now."

"I'll see to it now, Mayor," Beaumont said, and left the office.

TWENTY-EIGHT

Clint and Temple were in Pete Tanner's office, all making use of the editor's coffeepot.

"So what do I do now?" Temple asked Clint. "Just walk around and wait for him to kill me?"

"Not quite," Clint said, "but we are going to want you to be visible."

"So then he goes to saloons? Cafés?" Tanner asked.

"Well," Clint said, "first I have a feeling we'll be going to either City Hall or the police station."

"Ah, yes," Tanner said. "There are a couple of gentlemen who aren't gonna be very happy—and even less so tomorrow."

"Maybe," Clint said, "you should go and see them first, Mr. Tanner."

"For a statement," Tanner said, sitting up straight. "Now that the article is out there."

"Right."

"That's normally what I'd do after one of my pieces appears," Temple said.

"No," Clint said, "not until we find out what kind of mood they're in."

"And that's my job," Tanner said, standing up.

"I would suggest you don't rub it in," Clint said. "Just get a statement."

"Not rub it in?" Tanner asked. "Are you kidding? Any chance I get to make the mayor look bad is a godsend. Don't worry about me. I can handle politicians." He grabbed a notebook. "I'll see you fellas later!"

As Tanner almost ran from the room, Clint said, "Wow, he's eager."

"What's he going to do when tomorrow's piece comes out, I wonder," Temple said.

Chief Landry entered the mayor's office, hoping he'd be able to hold his temper. He wasn't looking to get fired from another job.

"Have a seat, W.T.," Stanley said.

Landry sat down, eyeing the mayor warily.

"So tell me," Stanley asked, "are you as lost as the newspaper says you are?"

Landry's face turned beet red, and yet he still fought to hold his temper. But before he could answer, the mayor continued.

"Because I'd hate to think so, W.T.," he said. "I'd really hate to think so."

"Mayor," Landry said, "we're not lost. We are using every asset available to us, including this reporter and Clint Adams. This killer is as good as caught."

"I want him caught, tried," the mayor said, "and hanged here."

"Well," the chief said, "I can catch him, but for the rest, you're going to need a judge."

"Don't worry," Stanley said, "I have a judge."

"Then I should get on with my job."

"Yes, you should," the mayor said.

The chief stood up.

"If anyone wants to talk about this—the reporter, or

Tanner, or Adams, or anyone else—refer them to me. Don't talk to anyone. Just do the job."

"All right, Mayor."

"When you pass Beaumont's office, tell him I want to see him."

"I will."

Stanley waved him away.

As the chief came to the district attorney's office, he stopped and thought a moment before entering. The man's secretary was not at her desk, so he bypassed it and went to the inner office. He knocked and entered.

"Chief!" Beaumont said. "Come on in."

Beaumont's desk was almost as large as the mayor's, but his office was smaller.

"Would you like a drink?"

"No," the chief said. "I just came from seeing the mayor. He wants to see you."

"Of course he does," Beaumont said. "He always wants to see me."

"Well, before you go," Landry said, "we should talk."

"Have a seat."

The chief sat. "Have you made up your mind?" he asked. "About running against him, I mean?"

"I have," Beaumont said. "I don't think I have much choice."

"Good."

"Have you heard of anyone else willing to run?"

"No."

"That's good. What did the mayor want with you?"

"He's upset about the article in the newspaper."

"Yes, he is."

"He wants the killer convicted and hanged here in Abilene. He'll need a judge for that."

"He has a judge," Beaumont said. "In fact, he has

more than one. So all that needs to be done is to catch the killer."

"My job," Landry said. "I know that. What I want to know is, after you're mayor, will I still have that job?"

Beaumont sat back in his chair and regarded the man.

"Do you know anyone better for the job?"

"No."

"Then that's your answer."

The chief nodded, and left.

Beaumont walked to the mayor's office. Mayor Stanley's rule was almost over, and his was still to start. But first they had to get past this problem. This one man who'd strangled one girl in Abilene had to be caught before he could strike again. For that he felt sure they had to depend on the Gunsmith. He would have to have a meeting with Clint Adams soon, without the mayor knowing about it.

But first he had to act like the loyal second in command. He opened the door and went inside.

TWENTY-NINE

Tanner heard footsteps behind him and turned to see Clint Adams coming toward him.

"What's this?" he asked.

"I decided I should come with you."

"And Temple?"

"He's going to stay in your offices," Clint said. "He has a gun. He should be safe."

"I hope so."

"This won't take long," Clint said. "Let's go see what kind of mood the administration is in."

At the police station they were told by the sergeant at the front desk that the chief was unavailable to talk to Mr. Tanner.

"He authorized me to say one thing to you," the sergeant said.

"What's that?" Tanner asked, getting ready to write it down.

The sergeant leaned forward and said slowly, "No . . . comment."

They left the police station and went to City Hall, where they got a better reception.

"Mr. Tanner," Ned Beaumont said when he spotted them in the hall. "Mr. Adams. Welcome." He was on his way back from the mayor's office.

"Mr. Beaumont," Pete Tanner said. "I was hoping to get a statement from the mayor about the story that's in today's paper."

"Yes, I'm sure you were," Beaumont replied, "but I think before you try to do that, we should go to my office and have a talk."

Tanner looked at Clint, who nodded.

"Good," Beaumont said. "Come with me."

He led the way to his office. There was still no secretary there. In point of fact, his secretary had left several days earlier to get married, and he had not yet been able to replace her.

"Please," he said inside his office, "have a seat, both of you."

They sat down as he went around behind his desk and did the same.

"What's on your mind, Mr. Beaumont?" Clint asked.

"We haven't sat down together since we played poker, Clint," Beaumont said. "You can call me Ned, though."

"Okay, Ned. What's this about?"

Beaumont looked at Tanner and said, "What I tell you now is off the record."

"Okay."

He addressed them both.

"The mayor is on his way out," he said. "I'm going to run against him in the next election."

"When is that?" Clint asked.

"Three months."

"You'll have to declare soon, and start campaigning," Tanner said.

"I know."

"What's that got to do with what's going on now?" Clint asked.

"I'll need help," Beaumont said. "Yours," he said to Clint, then looked at Tanner, "and your new reporter's."

Clint and Tanner exchanged a glance.

"What is it?" Beaumont asked, noticing something pass between the two.

"I think you'll be real interested in tomorrow's edition," Clint said.

THIRTY

Beaumont showed Clint and Tanner the way to the mayor's office.

"Wait out here," he said, and went inside.

The mayor looked up and said, "Back so soon?"

"Clint Adams is in the hall with Pete Tanner."

"Tanner! That bastard!"

"He wants a statement from you about the piece in today's paper."

Mayor Stanley's face turned red.

"Bring him in. I'll give him a statement."

Beaumont leaned on the desk.

"Mayor, calm down. It won't do any good to go off half-cocked. Not with an election around the corner."

"Yes, yes, you're right, damn it," Stanley said. He sat back in his chair and took a deep breath. "All right, let them in."

"Do you want me to come in with them?"

"No, no," Stanley said, "you've done enough, Ned. Just send them in and go back to your office."

"Yes, sir."

Beaumont came out of the mayor's office and joined Clint and Tanner in the hall.

"Okay, he's ready," he said. "I got him calmed down, but he could go crazy at any minute and start yelling. When he does that, there's no talking to him."

"Is he armed?" Clint asked.

"Only with a bad temper."

"Okay, then," Clint said, looking at Tanner, "let's go in."

They opened the door and entered.

By the time Clint Adams and Pete Tanner entered his office, Mayor Stanley had his temper under control—or so he thought. His temper was one of the things he had in common with Chief Landry—it was their previous acquaintance that had influenced him to hire the man, in spite of his checkered past.

He knew Landry struggled with his temper, just as he did, and now Stanley's temper flared as he saw Pete Tanner enter. He made a concerted effort to calm down again.

"Gentlemen," he said, "what can I do for you?"

The killer had an idea.

He had read the story in the newspaper while having breakfast in a small café. He set the paper aside to finish his food, and think. At that moment a young waitress came by with a pot of coffee.

"More coffee?"

"Please."

She refilled his cup, smiled at him, and walked away.

He wanted to kill her.

But he had a better idea.

Yes, he needed to kill a girl, but not this one. He had another in mind.

With Clint Adams and the reporter, Temple, in town to find him, it would be a daring thing to kill again. They were probably hoping to catch him before he struck again. Killing again now would be a slap in the face to them.

And to the Abilene police, and government.

It was too tempting to ignore.

He sipped his coffee and looked out the window at the dress shop across the street.

He had an idea.

"A comment," the mayor said.

"Yes," Tanner said.

"You want a comment from me on the piece in today's newspaper."

"That's right."

"Very well," the man said, taking a deep breath. Clint wondered if he was going to start yelling, but when he spoke, his voice was perfectly under control. "I think it was monumentally improper and careless. I can see why Mr. Temple got himself in trouble in Boston."

"But more than anything else, Mr. Temple has made himself a target," Tanner said. "What do you think of that?"

The mayor leaned forward.

"What makes you think the killer will try for him?" he asked. "Don't you think he's smart enough to see it as a trap?"

"I think he'll see Mr. Temple as the only man who can lead to his capture," Tanner said.

"By making us—my police—look foolish."

"Well . . ." Tanner said, aware that the piece in the next day's newspaper was even worse.

"Mr. Adams?" the mayor said. "What are your thoughts?"

"I did think the killer would go after Mr. Temple when he saw the newspaper," Clint said.

"What's changed your mind?"

"Apparently Temple doesn't know as much about him as I thought."

"If that's true," the mayor said, "then he won't go after him."

"No," Clint said, suddenly having a thought, "but he might do something else."

"Like what?" the mayor asked.

"He might make us all look bad," Clint said, "and strike again."

THIRTY-ONE

Clint and Tanner stopped just outside City Hall.

"That's a desperate man," Tanner said.

"Are you going to write that in your paper?"

"I'm going to wait and see what happens when tomorrow's edition comes out."

"So what are you going to do now?"

"I'm going back to my office."

"Okay, I'll walk with you," Clint said. "I want to make sure Temple didn't go anywhere."

They started walking.

"You think he's foolish enough to go anywhere without you?" Tanner asked.

"I hope not."

"Mr. Adams!"

Clint stopped and turned, saw Detective Stokes coming across the street toward him.

"Go ahead," he told Tanner. "I'll be there after I talk to Detective Stokes."

"Okay," Tanner said. "I'll tell Temple you'll be along."

"Right."

"That is, unless I can sit in on this little talk—"

"I don't think so, Pete."

"Yeah, okay."

Tanner walked on as Stokes reached Clint.

"Can we talk?"

"Here?"

Stokes looked around. There was a small saloon right across the street.

"How about there?"

"Isn't it a little early for beer?" Clint asked.

"It's never too early for beer," Stokes said.

"Okay, let's go."

They were the only two men in the saloon, leaning on the bar with a beer in front of each of them. The bartender had served them and then moved to the other end of the bar. Clint had a feeling the man knew who Stokes was. He hadn't asked for any money for the beers.

"What's on your mind, Detective?" Clint asked. "I suppose you read the newspaper today."

"I did," Stokes said. "I thought it was really funny."

"Funny?"

"He made the mayor and the chief look foolish," Stokes said. "Hell yeah, that's funny."

"You think that was funny, wait until you see tomorrow's edition."

"I can't wait," Stokes said, "but that's not what I'm here about."

"Oh," Clint said. "Then maybe you want to talk to me about those two idiots you had following me and Harry Temple."

"They were there for your protection."

"They were there to be seen, Detective."

"Well, yeah . . ."

"Why?"

"I wanted you to know that the chief doesn't trust you," Stokes said. "He wanted you watched. He told me to put my best men on it."

"So you picked those two, so I'd see them."

"Guilty."

"Well," Clint said, "I don't see them this morning."

"I sent them back to their regular jobs."

"And did you assign two more men?" Clint asked. "Men so good at their jobs that I haven't seen them . . . yet?"

"No," Stokes said, "not yet."

"Well, do me a favor and get it done."

"You mean you want me to have someone watch you?" Stokes asked.

"I need to have Temple protected."

"And here I thought that's what you were doing," the detective said.

"It's not always a one-man job, Detective."

"What did the mayor have to say?"

"He's not happy," Clint answered.

"No, he's not," Stokes said. "He made that very clear to the chief."

"And how do you know that?"

"Because when the mayor yells at the chief," Stokes said, "the chief yells at me. Wants to know why I haven't caught this killer yet."

"So you don't get along with your chief?" Clint asked. "Or you just don't like him?"

"Both."

"Then why work for him?"

"I may not be for much longer."

"Are you going to quit?" Clint asked.

"I prefer to think that the chief will get fired . . . by the new mayor."

"A new mayor?" Clint asked. "All I've heard since I got to Abilene is that nobody wants to run against the mayor."

"Well," Stokes said, "that used to be true. But things are changing."

Clint wondered if Sheriff Evans knew that things were changing.

"Anyway," Stokes said, "I didn't want to talk to you about the mayor. Can you tell me exactly what Temple knows about the killer? I got the feeling he was holding back."

"You know," Clint said, "I had that feeling, too, but guess what? He's not."

"Not what?"

"Holding back," Clint said. "He really doesn't know much about the man."

"But in Boston—"

"He found out a name the killer was going by," Clint said. "Printed it in the paper, and the man left town. End of story. Except that he felt so responsible he went on this two-year quest to find him again."

"And maybe he has."

"Maybe," Clint said, "but . . ."

"But what?"

"I just had a thought this morning that the piece in the paper might not have the effect we were looking for."

"You think he'll leave town?" Stokes said. "I mean, if he's ever still here."

"I think instead of leaving town—if he's still here—" Clint said, "or instead of trying to kill Temple, he might simply strike again."

"Kill another girl? To rub our noses in it?"

"That's my thought."

Stokes picked up his beer and said, "Jesus, I hope you're wrong about that."

Clint picked his up and said, "So do I, Detective. So do I."

THIRTY-TWO

When Clint got back to the office of the *Reporter-News*, the press was running. He found Tanner and Temple deep in conversation in the editor's office.

"Here he is," Tanner said.

"Pete says you talked with Stokes," Temple said. "What was that about?"

"He was just wondering what we were doing about finding the killer."

"Isn't that his job?" Temple asked.

"He thought you might know something that you were holding back."

"And did you tell him I'm not?"

"I did," Clint said.

"How did he take that?"

"Surprisingly well."

"Anything else?"

"He's going to be putting two more men on us," Clint said. "Better men this time."

"Why didn't he put better men in the first place?" Tanner asked.

"Because he wanted us to see them," Clint said.

"Why?" Tanner asked.

"Just as a warning," Clint said. "Apparently he wanted us to know that the chief doesn't trust us."

"And does he trust the chief?"

"Doesn't trust him," Clint said, "and doesn't like him. He seems to think the chief will lose his job when the new mayor comes on board."

"New mayor?" Tanner grabbed his notebook. "Did he say who he thought was gonna run?"

"He didn't."

"Can we talk?" Temple said to Clint. "In the back?"

"Sure."

As they started down the hall to the back, Clint heard Tanner muttering, "New mayor, new mayor . . ." as if trying to decide who that might be.

In Temple's closet-sized office he said, "Tanner told me what you said in the mayor's office."

"Which part?"

"About the killer maybe striking again to make us all look bad?"

"Oh, that."

"Do you really believe that?"

"It was just something that occurred to me at the moment."

"And you believe it?"

Clint hesitated. "I don't want to, but . . ."

"So maybe my having that piece in the newspaper will make him kill again?" Temple asked, eyes wide. "Jesus. This could be worse than Boston!"

"We don't know anything yet," Clint said. "And even if he does kill again, I don't think you can take the blame for that, Harry."

"No," Temple said, "no, I wouldn't take the blame. I'd blame you! You talked me into writing for the paper. And what about tomorrow's edition?"

"That's got nothing to do with the killer."

"No, only the most powerful men in Abilene."

"Well, that may not be for very long."

"Jesus . . ." Temple said, sitting down in his squeaky chair.

"Try to take it easy, Harry," Clint said. "The cards have been dealt. We just have to wait and see how the hand plays out."

"I'm not a gambler, Clint."

"Oh, really?" Clint asked. "You could have fooled me, Harry."

THIRTY-THREE

The killer stood across the street from Mathilda's Dress Shop, watching customers come and go, squinting against the dust kicked up by passing horses and wagons.

He might not have even thought about Mathilda had he not been able to see the store from the café window. And while most of the customers seemed to be middle-aged women, he did take a look in the window and see the young girl behind the counter.

Now he just stood watching the front of the store, going over the possibilities in his head. He certainly enjoyed thinking about this more than thinking about Clint Adams and the reporter, Temple.

When Clint decided that he and Temple should go out to get some air, the reporter balked.

"You just want me to walk around and make a target of myself," he accused.

"Look," Clint said, "so far we know two things. One, that the killer's victims are young women, and two, that he strangles them. Even if he decides to kill you, he's going to have to get close if he wants to strangle you."

"What about that shot the other night?"

"I'm starting to think that wasn't him."

"I don't know . . ."

By the time Clint convinced the young man, it was time to have some lunch . . .

Clint decided to try the small café across the street from Mathilda's Dress Shop. He'd seen it several times, but had not yet been there.

There were several tables available, and they got the one that was the farthest from the front window.

"What's good here?" Temple asked.

"I've never been here before."

"Then why did you pick it?"

"I want to try it," Clint said. "Besides, I have a friend who works across the street."

"The general store?"

"The dress shop."

"Ah . . ."

Clint decided on the beef stew, and Temple simply told the waiter to bring him the same.

While they weren't seated at the window, they could still see outside from where they sat.

"Looks like a busy little store," Temple said.

"She does all right."

"I guess she knows what these women like to wear, huh?" Temple asked. "Probably because she's one of them?"

"One of what?"

"These middle-aged ladies."

"Uh, no," Clint said, "she's younger than that."

"Oh," Temple said. "Well, I thought you were implying something romantic."

"What if I was?"

"Uh, well, I thought, you know, you being your age, and all, that she wouldn't be . . . you know, that young."

Clint glared across the table.

"How old do you think I am? No, wait," he said before Temple could reply. "Don't answer that."

The waiter came with their bowls and they both leaned back to allow him to serve.

"Look," Temple said, "I didn't mean anything. I just thought, you know, you being this legend of the West and all, that you were . . ."

"Old?"

"Well."

"Just eat your stew!"

The killer was surprised.

When he saw Clint Adams and Harry Temple enter the café just across the street from where he was standing, he worried—just for a moment—that they knew he was there. But then he decided it had to be a coincidence. In fact, if they'd arrived earlier, while he was still inside the same café, it would have been a *hell* of a coincidence.

In the end he decided there was no harm in remaining right where he was. They had inadvertently given him more than one choice as to how to spend the rest of his afternoon.

"The stew was good," Temple said as they waited for coffee and pie.

Clint grunted.

"Come on," Temple said, "I didn't mean anything by it."

"Yeah, all right."

"It's the reputation, you know?" Temple said. "That kind of thing, it ages you."

"Yeah."

"Unless you're, you know, Billy the Kid, or somebody like that."

"I knew Billy."

Temple dropped his fork and said, "Aw, come on . . ."

THIRTY-FOUR

As they finished their pie, Clint told stories of Billy the Kid, Jesse James, and Wyatt Earp.

"Probably my best friend of them all is Bat Masterson," Clint said. "And then there's Talbot Roper."

"Who?"

"He's a private detective who works out of Denver. Used to be a Pinkerton."

"Did you know Allan Pinkerton?"

"Better than I wanted to," Clint admitted.

"You know," Temple said, "if you ever wanted to write a book—"

"That's been suggested before," Clint said. "I don't want to write a book. Or—before you ask—have a book written about me."

"Even if you did," Temple said, "you'd probably go to Mark Twain and ask him to do it."

"No," Clint said, "I wouldn't."

Temple took that to mean he still had a chance. His eyes lit up.

"Well, if you ever change your mind—"

"I won't."

Clint ate the last hunk of pie.

*   *   *

Mattie happened to be looking out her window when Clint Adams and a younger man walked into the café across the street. She kept her eyes on the café after that, and when she saw them come out again, she hurriedly left the store, even though there were a couple of customers there.

She waved and ran across the street.

Clint saw Mattie come out, wave, and start running toward them.

"Hey," Temple said. "Is that her?"

"Yes, that's her."

"Wow," the reporter said, "she's young . . . a-and pretty," he added hurriedly.

"Clint!"

Mattie stumbled stepping up onto the boardwalk, fell into Clint, who caught her.

"Oh! Thank you," she said. "I saw you go into the café. Is everything all right?"

"Yes, it's fine, Mattie," Clint said. "This is Harry Temple."

"Mr. Temple."

"Ma'am."

"You boys could have asked me about this place," she said. "I would've told you it was fine. I have lunch here quite often."

"It was," Temple stammered, "uh, fine, I mean."

"Well, good," she said. She looked at Clint. "Is he the one—"

"Yes," Clint said, cutting her off, "he's the one, but you should go back to work, Mattie. I told you, it isn't safe to be around me—around us—right now."

"All right, all right," she said, backing away, "I just wanted to say hello."

Clint grabbed her before she stumbled off the boardwalk backward, into the path of a passing buckboard.

"Oops, thanks."

"You better get back before you hurt yourself," Clint told her.

"You're right." She touched his chest. "I'll see you later." Then she looked at Temple. "It was nice to meet you, Mr. Temple."

"Uh, y-you, too, ma'am."

She looked at Clint again and said, "He's cute," and then ran back across the street.

"Harry, don't tell me," Clint said. "You're shy around women."

"Just pretty women, like her," Temple said. "How did you guess?"

"Come on," Clint said. "We've stayed in one place for too long."

The killer watched the encounter between Clint, Temple, and the girl, who might or might not have been named Mathilda. He was able to recognize what passed between Clint Adams and the girl. And the girl—well, she was just very special, perfect for him.

He watched as they talked, and then the girl ran back across to her store.

Adams and Temple spoke for a moment, and then started walking down the street. The killer had a choice— follow them or stay and wait for the girl to come out.

It was a fairly easy decision for him to make.

THIRTY-FIVE

The rest of the day went pretty much without incident. Two more policemen appeared to watch Clint and Temple. They were better than the other two, but Clint was still able to spot them.

In the office, Temple asked, "Does that mean they're terrible at it, too? I mean, since you saw them?"

"No," Clint said, "I'm just that good. Stokes assured me that these are better men. In case of an emergency, they'll be helpful."

"That's good to hear."

Tanner came down the hall from his office.

"I'm going home," he said. "Tomorrow's edition is ready. Do you want to see it?"

"No," Temple said, "that's okay. I know what I wrote."

"Suit yourself."

"Tanner," Temple said.

"Yeah?"

"You're not going to get . . . burned out or anything because of it, are you?"

"Don't worry," Tanner said. "I've got the money to rebuild if they do."

"Rebuild?"

"I'm financing this newspaper on my own," Tanner said. "There's no way they can put me out of business."

"That's good to know," Clint said.

"Good night," the editor said. "See you two in the morning."

"Yeah, good night," Temple said.

After Tanner left, Clint said, "Let's get a beer and then some supper."

"Really?" Temple said. "Go to a saloon? Isn't that kind of . . . public?"

"You can't really be bait if you're not in public," Clint pointed out.

"Well . . . we did say this might not work."

"Yes, we did."

"Okay," Temple said, "let's get a beer."

They decided on the Big Horn Saloon, which was crowded, but not to the point where they couldn't find places at the bar.

"Two beers," Clint said to the bartender.

"Comin' up."

With beers in hand, they turned and looked over the saloon.

"He could be in here," Temple said.

"Yes, he could."

"Or he could be gone."

"That, too."

Temple took a swallow of beer, then turned and looked at Clint.

"Have I wasted two years?"

"What do you mean?"

"I mean, I've been following him—trying to follow him—for two years, and what do I have to show for it?"

"Well, it all may come to an end here," Clint said.

"Yeah, but what if it doesn't?" Temple said. "What do I do then?"

"I guess that would depend on how badly you want to see him caught."

Temple frowned.

"Maybe not as badly as two years ago," he said. "That's a hard thing to admit."

"Harry," Clint said, "you could just go back home and resume your life. Nobody's going to think badly of you."

"I wouldn't go back to Boston," Temple said, "but maybe somewhere else. New York. Philadelphia."

"I'm sure a newspaper back there would be glad to have you."

"Writing again, even for a small paper in Abilene, did feel good," Temple admitted. "But if he kills again—"

"We already established that you couldn't take all the blame for that," Clint said, cutting him off, "even if you wanted to."

"Yeah," Temple said, "we did, didn't we?"

"Just relax and finish your beer," Clint said. "You don't have to decide anything now."

"I guess not."

"Let's get another one," Clint said, turning back to the bar and waving to the bartender.

The killer was surprised by two things. First, she didn't come out of the store until it started to get dark. Second, she didn't have far to go apparently. All she did was walk around the corner. He was hoping to grab her off the street, but instead he had to hurry to come up behind her on the steps leading to her rooms.

"Wha—" she started, but he cut her off by slapping his hand over her mouth.

"If you scream," he said, "I'll kill you. Understand?"

She nodded, eyes wide.

He pushed her the rest of the way upstairs and said, "Unlock the door."

She tried to say something, so he had to remove his hand to understand her.

"It's n-not locked."

"Of course it's not," he said. "All right, inside."

He pushed her in and followed, pulling the door shut behind him . . . and locking it.

THIRTY-SIX

Clint slept well.

No one came to his door, not even Mathilda, which was good. She needed to stay away from him, and he needed to get a good night's sleep.

So there was no knock on his door . . . until morning.

The sun had been streaming through his window for a couple of hours when the knock came. At that hour he doubted it was Mathilda. Maybe Temple. When it became more insistent, he grabbed his gun and went to the door.

"Who is it?"

"Detective Stokes sent me."

He unlocked the door and opened it an inch. He recognized the man in the hall as one of the new cops watching him and Temple.

"What is it?" he asked.

"You better get dressed and come with me, Mr. Adams," the policeman said.

"What's going on?"

"You'll see."

"You better wake Temple."

"My partner is doing that," the man said. "We'll wait in the lobby."

* * *

Clint and Temple came out into the hall at the same time and headed for the stairs.

"Do you know what this is about?" Temple asked.

"No," Clint said, "just that Stokes wants us."

"Do you think—"

"I'm trying not to think," Clint said.

The two policemen were waiting in the lobby. They said that their names were Bishop and Odon, and that they had a buggy out front to drive Clint and Temple to the scene. They didn't say scene of *what*.

But as soon as they came within sight of Mathilda's Dress Shop, Clint said, "Oh, no."

"What is it?" Temple asked, but then he also noticed where they were.

The buggy stopped. Clint stepped down and asked Odon, "Where is she?"

"Upstairs."

He ran for the stairs, and Temple followed. At the top he found Stokes waiting for him.

"Mathilda Lawson—" he started to say, but Clint cut him off.

"I know her."

"Oh," Stokes said. "I'm sorry . . ."

Clint moved past him into the room. She was lying on her back on the floor. She looked like she was sleeping, except for the mottled skin around her neck and the tip of her tongue sticking out. Beside her lay a bright orange neckerchief.

"Damnit!" he swore.

"This is different," Stokes said. "He grabbed the other one off the street and left her in an alley." He looked at Temple. "How did it go in Boston?"

"The same," Temple said, cutting him off. "He'd grab them from the street, and then leave them somewhere else on a street or in an alley."

"So then," Stokes said, "maybe this isn't the same killer. Maybe—"

"It's him," Clint said. "He used an orange scarf to strangle her." Clint looked at Stokes. "He's sending us a message. Somehow he knew I knew her, and he couldn't resist."

"So instead of coming after Temple, he went after her?" Stokes said.

"Damnit!" Temple swore.

Clint knew what he was thinking.

"It's not your fault, Harry," he said.

"Yeah, well, that's easy to say . . ." He shook his head and went back outside.

"Why does he feel it's his fault?"

"The piece in the newspaper," Clint said. "He thinks he pushed the killer into this."

"I hate to say it," Stokes said, "but maybe he's right."

"Killers kill, Detective," Clint said. "They don't have to be pushed into it."

"You sound experienced."

"With killers? Very."

"Sure, gunfighters, Indians, but what about this?" Stokes said. "Stranglers like this?"

"One in England, one in Seattle . . . yeah, I've seen this before. Nobody has to make them kill. They like it too much to need help doing it."

"But this one," Stokes said. "It may not be his fault, but—"

"Go ahead, say it," Clint said. "It may be mine. He picked her to send me a message. That doesn't make it my fault, Detective. The fault is still all his."

Stokes shrugged, impressed at Clint Adams's attitude about the murder.

"But that doesn't mean I'm not going to catch him," Clint said, "because I am. I swear to you, I am."

THIRTY-SEVEN

Clint and Temple stayed on the street in front of the building until Stokes had the body removed.

"Anybody see anything?" Clint asked him.

"That's what I'm going to have my men asking," Stokes said.

Clint was about to say something else when he saw Sheriff Evans approaching. Stokes saw him at the same time.

"Oh, no," he said, "that old-time badge-toter. What's he want?"

"He probably wants to help," Clint said. "If you let him, you'd find out he's probably a good man. And he's known these people a long time."

Clint moved to intercept Evans.

"Not Mattie," Evans said.

"I'm afraid so."

"Jesus," he said, shaking his head. "First Laurie, and now . . . that sonofabitch!"

"Mattie didn't say anything to me about someone watching her," Clint said. "Did she mention it to you?"

"No," Evans said, "and I just saw her yesterday. She did talk about you, though."

"Me?"

He nodded.

"She wanted to know how long I thought you'd be stayin' around. I guess she liked you."

"Well, I liked her," Clint said. "I'm going to catch that sonofabitch, you can depend on that."

"I'd like to help, if they'll let me," Evans said.

"Talk to Detective Stokes over there," Clint said. "I'm sure he'll welcome your help."

"You think so?"

"I do."

Sheriff Evans left Clint and walked over to Detective Stokes. Clint watched the big detective turn to face Evans, and then the two shook hands. At that point Temple came walking over to him.

"I'm so sorry, Clint."

"Yeah, but not half as sorry as this killer's going to be," Clint said. "You can depend on that."

"So where do we start?"

"Somebody around here had to have seen something," Clint said.

"Clint, he's never been seen grabbing a girl," Temple reminded him.

"But he had to watch her for a while, right? Figure out when to grab her? Somebody might have seen him standing around, keeping an eye on the store."

"Aren't the police going to ask?"

"They're going to be looking for someone who actually saw him take her," Clint said, "but like you said, he's never been seen."

"Can't you get them to act differently?"

"Detective Stokes strikes me as a man who has to follow his known procedure. That's where he's at a disadvantage, no matter how good he is at his job."

"So we have an advantage."

"We do."

"That's good to know. So should we split up?"

"No." Clint looked across the street, where a crowd had gathered to watch. "He could be any one of those men. We better stay together, where I can keep an eye on you."

"I'm not going to argue with that."

"Besides," Clint said, "the mayor and the chief have read the newspaper by now. One of them might come after you."

"You know," Temple said, "I forgot all about that."

"They're not going to forget it," Clint said. "That's for damn sure."

THIRTY-EIGHT

Clint decided to simply work the side of the street across from the store, starting with the café he and Temple had eaten in. They talked to all the waiters, then to the people in the stores on either side.

"You know," said the owner of the photographic studio to the right of the café, "there was a fella loitering out front for most of yesterday."

"Yesterday?"

"Yeah, in the afternoon. I had the feeling he came out of the café next door, but then stayed around, watching . . . something."

"Watching what?" Clint asked.

"I don't know," the balding man said, "something across the street." He was in his mid-forties, wearing a long leather apron and smelling faintly of chemicals.

"You didn't happen to take his picture, did you?" Clint asked.

"Naw," the man said, "why would I have done that?"

"Of course," Clint said, "why would you have?"

"But I did take a picture," the man went on, "up here." He pointed to his head. "I got that kind of memory."

"That's great," Clint said. "What did he look like?"

The photographer gave them a description of the man that was almost as good as a picture.

"I hope that helps," the man said. "If you don't mind, I have some business inside."

"Of course," Clint said. "Thanks a lot."

The photographer went back inside.

"Now what?"

"Have you ever had this much information about the killer before?"

"No."

"We don't have a picture, but we have something almost as good."

"So where do we start?"

"Next door," Clint said. "The café again. Now that we can describe him, maybe somebody in there saw him and heard a name."

They went back to the café to question the waiters. Across the street, the killer stood with his arms folded, leaning against a wall, blending in with other onlookers who were now lining both sides of the street. He felt great satisfaction in having policemen all around him, as well as Clint Adams and the reporter, Temple.

He wondered, though, why Adams and Temple were going back into the café after having already been there. His gaze shifted over to the store he'd been standing in front of when he was watching Mathilda's Dress Shop. At the time, he had not realized it was a photography studio.

He wondered if the photographer had told them anything damaging. He'd have to ask the man, but that would have to wait until all the commotion had died down, and the onlookers moved along.

He could wait.

"Oh yeah," a young waitress said, "I remember that feller. He had the beef stew." She was the only waitress who worked in the café. The others were waiters.

"You remember anything else about him?"

"Well . . . he was a pretty finicky eater, always wiping his mouth with his napkin. And, oh yeah, he spent a lot of time starin' out the window."

"Did he talk to you about anything other than eating?" Clint asked.

"No," the waitress said, "he only spoke to me to order, or to ask for something else."

"Did you see where he went when he left?" Clint asked.

"No, sir," the waitress said. "I had other tables to wait on. I just seen him go out the door."

"Did he looks at you, uh, kind of funny?" Temple asked.

"Whataya mean, funny?"

"Did he make you uncomfortable?"

"Well . . ."

"What's your name?" Clint asked.

"Heather."

"It's okay, Heather," he said. "You can tell us."

"He . . . uh, did make me feel uncomfortable when he first came in. Staring at me. He touched my arm once, when I served him his stew. Gave me the willies. But then . . . I don't know, he started staring out the window. After that he stopped. Didn't seem to notice me at all, unless he wanted something."

Clint stared out the window at what the killer would have been seeing, and saw the front of Mathilda's Dress Shop.

"Okay, Heather," Clint said. "Thank you."

"Did I help?"

"Yes, Heather," he said, "you helped us quite a bit."

Outside, Temple said, "She helped?"

"She did."

"How?"

Clint pointed at the dress shop.

"That's what the killer saw when he stared out the

window," he said. "I think he saw Mathilda, and forgot about lucky little Heather."

"Ah . . ."

"And one more thing just occurred to me."

"What's that?"

"First, we probably just missed him in the café when we ate," Clint said.

"And?"

"And if he was around here all afternoon, watching," Clint said, "then he might have seen her talking to us."

"Ah," Temple said, "I see what you mean."

"Come on," Clint said, "we'll talk to some more people on this side of the street. Somebody else might have seen something."

"What about Stokes?"

"What about him?"

"Are you going to tell him what we found out?" Temple asked.

"Yes," Clint said, "but only after we find out some more."

THIRTY-NINE

Clint and Temple spent the next few hours talking to people in the area. They were told that although the police had questioned them already, they had not asked the same questions.

"We're working on some different ideas," Clint said.

They were finished and had decided to go the saloon for a beer when they saw Stokes coming toward them.

"Do you want to tell him now?" Temple asked.

"Let's see what he has to say first."

The crowd on both sides of the street had thinned out. Clint did not see any of Stokes's uniformed men on the street at all.

"Detective," Clint said. "Have you found out anything?"

"Yeah," Stokes said, "either nobody saw anything, or nobody wants to say they saw anything."

"That's too bad."

"Yeah, it is," Stokes said. "I'll tell you what else is too bad. That article this fella wrote in the newspaper today."

"What about it?" Temple asked.

"The chief went off like a steam engine this morning," Stokes said. "And I hear the mayor did the same."

"Sounds like it had the desired effect, then," Temple said.

"Chief Landry wants me to bring you in," Stokes said to Temple.

"For what?"

"Questioning."

"Again," Temple said, "for what?"

"He says he thinks maybe you know something about this latest murder."

"He's crazy—"

"No, he's mad," Stokes said, "and he wants to make things tough on you."

"Are you going to take him in?" Clint asked.

"I'm not," Stokes said, "on one condition."

"What's that?"

Stokes poked Clint in the chest with a thick forefinger. Clint thought he might find a bruise there later.

"Find me that killer," he said. "I've seen you walking up and down this street, talking to people. What makes me think you're asking them a whole different set of questions? And what makes me think maybe you got some of the answers you're looking for?"

"Detective—"

"Never mind," Stokes said. "Just make sure I don't see this young fella's face again unless you've got the killer with you." He looked at Temple. "I'm gonna tell the chief I couldn't find you. Keep it that way."

"Yes, sir," Temple said.

"Thanks, Stokes."

"Don't thank me," Stokes said to Clint. "Just don't make me look like a fool. If you do, I'll toss both your asses in jail."

"Got it," Clint said.

Stokes started to walk away, then stopped short and turned back.

"Oh, and I think you were right about Sheriff Evans,"

Stokes said. "I think he is a good man. Maybe even good enough to help you out."

"I think so, too," Clint said. "Thanks, Stokes."

The detective nodded and walked away.

"Are we going to the saloon?" Temple asked.

"Later," Clint said. "Let's go and talk to the sheriff. I think Stokes might be right."

"I don't know him," Temple said, "so I guess I'll take your word for it."

"You'll find out," Clint said. "Come on."

When they got to the sheriff's office, the lawman wasn't there. That alone indicated to Clint that the sheriff might have had a change of heart.

"What now?" Temple asked.

"Let's wait," Clint said. "He'll be back."

"Does he have any deputies?"

"No," Clint said, "just him."

"Why does the town need him if it has a police department?" Temple asked.

"I think that question is on the sheriff's mind, too," Clint said. "He'd like to make the town realize they do need him."

Clint went to the stove and checked the coffeepot. It was empty.

Temple walked to the doorway to the cell block and looked inside at the three cells. They were empty.

"Aren't the town sheriffs going away with the coming of the new decade?" Temple asked.

"Don't talk like that around Evans," Clint said. "Not if we want him to help us."

"So you're not any happier than he is that the Old West is becoming modernized."

"No, I'm not."

"Are you afraid you won't be able to make the transition?"

Clint stared at Temple and asked, "Why does this sound like an interview?"

Temple looked sheepish and said, "Oh, sorry."

"The turn of the century is coming for all of us, Harry," Clint said. "There's not much we can do about it, is there?"

"I guess not."

The door opened at that moment and Sheriff Evans walked in. He stopped short when he saw them, then came the rest of the way in and closed the door.

"You could've made coffee," he said.

"Didn't know where the makings were," Clint said.

"Well," Evans said, "if you fellas are gonna stay, I'll make some."

"Sounds good," Clint said.

"What brings you here?" Evans said, opening a cabinet and taking out a sack of coffee.

"We need to talk," Clint said. "We have some information, but we don't want to give it to the police."

"Clint would rather give it to you," Temple said. "He says you're a good man."

"He says that, huh?" He poured some water in the pot, then dropped in a few handfuls of coffee. Clint was glad to see that. The coffee would be plenty strong.

"Then I guess we should siddown and talk about some things, huh?"

FORTY

The smell of coffee quickly filled the room as Evans sat down behind his desk.

"I hear the chief and the mayor are on the warpath," he said.

"That's what we heard," Clint said.

"So you're hidin' out here?"

"For a while," Clint said. "Stokes sort of already warned us off."

"Yeah, I talked to him," Evans said. "He don't seem like such a bad guy."

"He said the same about you," Temple said. "Kind of."

"So what can I do for you fellas?" Evans asked.

"Pour us some of that coffee," Clint suggested, "and we'll talk about it."

Evans heaved himself up out of his chair and said, "Comin' up."

"Stokes!"

Stokes was expecting to hear the chief roar his name, so he reacted immediately.

"Sir?" he asked, coming through the office door.

"You find that reporter yet?"

"No, sir."

"I want his carcass in here today!" Landry said, his face almost purple with rage.

"I understand, sir," Stokes said. "I was just going out to look again."

"If you don't find his ass and drag it in here," Landry yelled after him, "don't bother coming back!"

Clint, Temple, and Evans sat around the office with steaming coffee mugs in their hands.

". . . so we have this mental image of the killer," Clint said, "and we know he was in the café yesterday afternoon."

"And in front of the photography studio," Temple added.

"Do you think he was around this mornin'," Evans asked, "watchin'?"

"I'm sure of it."

"Then he saw you questionin' people," Evans said. "Questioning the photographer—Ed Morgan by the way."

"He probably did," Temple said.

"Damn," Clint said.

"Yeah," Evans said. They both set down their mugs and stood up.

"What is it?" Temple asked.

"The photographer," Clint said. "He might be in trouble."

Temple hastily set his mug down as they headed for the door, and said, "Wait for me!"

When they got to the photography studio, the front door was locked.

"That's bad," Evans said. "He's usually open at this time of day."

"Maybe he had a job somewhere?" Clint suggested.

"He'd put a sign on his door saying when he'd be back," Evans said. "Ed doesn't want to lose any business."

Clint tried to see through the window into the interior of the shop.

"Anything?" Evans asked.

"I don't see anybody," Clint said.

"Should we try the back door?" Temple asked.

"To hell with that," the sheriff said. "Let's force the front."

Clint and Evans pressed their shoulders to the door. It slammed open, shattering the glass, but that was the least of their worries.

The three of them filed in and started looking around. Clint found Ed Morgan in his back room.

"Sheriff! Harry!"

"Damnit!" Evans said, fearing the worst. He and Temple went to the doorway that led to the back room, looked at each other, and went through.

Ed Morgan was lying on the floor on his back. Clint was crouching down next to him.

"Dead?" Evans asked.

"I'm afraid so."

"How?" Temple asked.

"Stabbed," Clint said, "looks like in the back."

"Not strangled?" Temple asked.

"No." Clint stood up. The three of them stood there, looking down.

"Now what?" Temple asked.

"We have to send for the police," Clint said.

"But—" Temple started.

"I know," Clint said. "We can't be here when they arrive."

They both looked at Evans.

"Yeah, okay," the sheriff said, "get out of here. Meet me at my office."

"We owe you, Sher—" Clint started.

"Yeah, yeah," Evans said. "Just get out of here."

FORTY-ONE

Clint and Temple waited for Sheriff Evans at his office, hoping nobody else would walk in. They finished the coffee in the pot and then Clint made another. It took hours, but Evans finally returned, and Clint handed him a cup of coffee.

"Thanks," he said. "Well, Stokes wasn't happy, and I'm not sure he believed that I just happened to go to the studio to question Ed. But in the end he accepted it."

"So now what?" Temple asked. "He was our only witness."

"He told us what he saw," Clint said. "It's not as if there was something he could have testified to in court."

"So I repeat, what do we do now?"

"Abilene has grown too big," Evans said. "It's not like we can go out on the street and try to match the description we have."

Temple looked over at Clint, who seemed to be deep in thought.

"Okay," he said, "what are you thinking?"

Clint looked at Evans.

"Do you know any artists in town?"

"Not me," he said. "You'd be better off asking Tanner about that."

"You're right."

"I think I know where you're headed," Temple said.

"Can somebody tell me?" Evans asked.

"I'm thinking of giving the photographer's description to an artist, and then printing the sketch in the newspaper."

"If you do that," Evans said, "the killer is gonna leave town."

"And if we can watch the roads leading out of town, we might spot him."

"On the other hand," Temple said, "that actually might make him come after us."

"But he kills women," Evans said.

"He already broke that pattern by killing Ed Morgan," Clint pointed out.

Evans shrugged, conceding that point to Clint.

"You think Tanner will agree to it?" Evans asked. "Doesn't he have enough trouble after your first two articles?"

"He's in trouble?" Temple asked.

"You didn't hear?" Evans asked.

"Hear what?"

"The mayor is closing the newspaper down."

"He can't do that," Temple said.

"He can if he keeps anybody from ever buying the paper."

Temple looked at Clint, who shook his head. If the sheriff didn't know that Tanner funded the newspaper himself, who were they to tell him?

"So," Evans went on, "if you want to get a sketch into that newspaper, you better hurry."

"He's right," Clint said. "Let's go. Sheriff, thanks for your help."

"Let me know what else I can do."

"We will," Clint said.

"Sure, I know an artist," Tanner said.

"Good," Clint said. "If we get a sketch, will you run it?"

"I will."

"What about your trouble?" Temple asked. Tanner looked at him. "The sheriff told us."

"The mayor can make it illegal to read my paper if he wants," Tanner said, "but I'll still put it out there. Don't worry about me."

"Okay," Clint said. "We have to stay off the street. Find your artist and bring him here, and we'll get started."

"I know just where he is," Tanner said, grabbing his hat. "I'll be right back."

FORTY-TWO

Clint and Temple were confusing the artist.

"Look," the young man said, "this would go better if only one of you talked."

Temple shrugged and said to Clint, "Go ahead."

The artist's name was Leo Wilkins. Clint recognized him because he worked at the livery stable, but Tanner said he was a talented artist.

"I use him for the paper sometimes—like today."

So Leo listened intently while Clint gave him the description that the photographer had given them. When he was done, they had a sketch of a man's face that seemed very clear.

"Is that him?" Leo asked.

Clint looked at the picture and said, "I hope so. Thanks, Leo."

"I hope it helps."

Clint took out some money and handed it to him.

"Thanks," Leo said, and left to go back to work at the livery. Tanner walked him out.

"Don't worry," he said when he came back. "He's not going to talk to anyone."

"Here," Clint said, handing him the sketch, "do whatever it is you do with this to put it in the paper."

"It'll be out tomorrow morning."

Clint nodded.

"And in the meantime?" Temple asked.

"We stay out of sight," Clint said.

"At the hotel?"

"No, if the mayor or the chief wants us badly enough, they'll go to the hotel."

"Here," Tanner said, handing Clint a key, "go to my house. There's food there, and an extra room. You fellas can stay there until the morning, when the edition comes out."

"That's as good a place as any," Clint said. "Thanks."

The editor gave them directions to his house, then went to work after they left.

"No sign of them," the chief told the mayor.

Mayor Stanley stood up from his desk and pointed his finger at Chief Landry.

"You better find them, Chief, or this is the last time you'll be called that."

"Yes, sir."

Angrily, Landry left the mayor's office, running into Ned Beaumont before he left City Hall.

"You better find them, W.T.," Beaumont said.

"You got any ideas how?"

"Your man Stokes."

"I'm not so sure he's my man," Landry said. "I think he might have his own agenda."

"Don't we all?" Beaumont said. "Do the best you can, Chief. I know you'll get it done."

"Thanks for the vote of confidence, Ned."

As the chief left, the district attorney went back to his own office.

The killer looked up as the door opened.

"What are you doing in my office?" the man demanded, glaring at the intruder, who was sitting in a visitor's chair.

"I wondered when you'd come back."

"I told you not to come here," the man said, moving around behind his desk and sitting down. "That's our agreement."

"Our agreement has changed."

"Yes, it has," the man said, "now that you've killed another girl. I told you to wait."

"I couldn't wait any longer."

"Too bad," the man said, "because now you've put us in a bad position."

"*Tsk tsk*," the killer said. "You know, when I came to Abilene and we met, I thought I'd found a kindred spirit."

The man behind the desk looked at the killer. Not a kindred spirit exactly, but someone who saw the killer for what he was, and thought he had a use for him.

"When you killed Laurie, I didn't mind—much," he said. "And I let you take a shot at the Gunsmith and his partner just for the fun of it. But we agreed no more until—"

"Until you found another use for me," the killer said. "But you took your time, so—"

"So you killed Mathilda. And now everyone's after you with renewed vigor."

"I don't mind," the killer said. "You'll think of something. You're a smart man. You don't become district attorney without being smart."

"Mayor," Ned Beaumont said. "I'm going to be mayor. And for that, I thought I'd need a man like you."

"If you could control me," the killer said.

"Yes."

"And now you know you can't."

"Can't I?"

The killer stood up. "Those men you promised me?"

"They're waiting in the Red Queen Saloon," Beaumont said. "Talk to a man named Mick, tell him I sent you."

"And they'll do what I tell them?"

"They will," Beaumont said. "You're going to have to really take care of Clint Adams and the reporter this time."

"I know that," the killer said. "I've known it all along."

"And then we can get back on track."

"Well," the killer said, moving around the desk, "I think your track and my track have sort of been . . . derailed."

Beaumont looked up at the killer, pushed his chair back in alarm, and said, "What do you—"

He got no further.

FORTY-THREE

When Tanner didn't come to his house that night, Clint got worried.

"He's probably just working late," Temple said, "getting tomorrow's edition out."

"He said he'd come home."

"He told me he spends a lot of nights in his office when he's working," Temple said.

He collected from the table the plates from their meager meal and carried them into the kitchen. When he came back into the living room, Clint was looking out the window.

"If you're that worried, let's go look for him."

"Now you're talking," Clint said.

When they got to the newspaper office, the front door was wide open.

"That's not a good sign," Clint said.

They went inside, found the place in shambles. The printing press had been smashed, and the place was strewn with broken furniture, shattered glass, and torn paper.

"The only thing they didn't do was burn the place down," Temple said.

"Tanner!" Clint said.

"His office."

They ran back to the editor's office, but it was in the same condition, completely destroyed.

"The killer?" Temple asked.

"I don't see any blood," Clint said, looking around. "And more than one man did this."

"So either the killer had help, or the mayor sent some men to destroy this place."

"But why would they take Tanner?" Clint asked.

"I guess there's one way to find out," the reporter said.

Clint nodded and said, "We ask him."

They didn't know where the mayor lived, so they went to City Hall. "We'll break in if we have to, and find his address."

"We could ask the sheriff," Temple said.

"Let's leave him out of this for now," Clint said.

Clint tried the front door and found it unlocked.

"Another bad sign," Temple said.

"Not necessarily," Clint said. "He might just be working late."

They opened the door and entered. The large building felt very empty. Standing just inside the door, in the entry foyer, they didn't hear a sound.

"Let's check the mayor's office," Clint said.

They went upstairs, made their way to Mayor Stanley's office, and entered. It was empty.

"Check his desk," Clint said. "See if you can find anything that tells us where he lives."

Temple went to the desk, while Clint looked around the rest of the room. There were some file cabinets, but they were locked. A small bar with expensive-looking bottles of liquor. A small writing desk in a corner, with nothing on it or in it.

"Here's an envelope addressed to him," Temple said.

"At City Hall?"

"No, another address in town."

"That's got to be it," Clint said.

At that moment they heard a door close in the hall and then footsteps. Clint held his hand out to Temple to be quiet. He put his hand on his gun, and they waited. The footsteps came closer, and then the mayor entered and stopped short.

"What the hell are you doing here?"

"Where did you just come from?" Clint demanded.

"The water closet, if it's any of your business."

"Where's Pete Tanner?"

"How should I know?"

"His office was ransacked and he's missing," Temple said. "Are you going to tell us you know nothing about that?"

"That's exactly what I'm going to tell you." For a big man he moved quickly across the room and snatched the envelope from Temple's hand. "Now get out!"

"If you didn't send men to wreck his office and grab him, who did?"

"How would I know?"

"Beaumont?" Clint asked. "Did you have your district attorney do it?"

"Mr. Beaumont has an agenda of his own," Stanley said. "Why don't you go and ask him?"

"We will," Clint said, "and you're coming with us."

When the three of them entered Beaumont's office, the mayor stopped short and said, "Oh my God."

Clint moved to the desk, where Beaumont was slumped, and checked the body.

"He's dead."

"Strangled?" Temple asked.

Clint shook his head and looked down at the pool of blood on the floor. "Stabbed."

"What the hell—" Mayor Stanley said. "Who did this?"

"The same man who killed the two girls and Ed Morgan."

"The killer we've been looking for," Temple said. "And it looks like he's just getting warmed up."

"But . . . why kill Beaumont?" the mayor asked.

"We'll ask the killer when we find him," Clint said.

"I think you might find your answer at the Red Queen Saloon," the mayor said, staring at Beaumont's body.

"Why there?" Clint asked.

"It's over the deadline," Stanley said. "Ned had a weakness for it. I can only think that the reason he's dead has something to do with that place."

Clint looked at Temple.

"Sounds like the kind of place our boy might like," Clint said.

"I—I guess we better check it out, then," Temple said, not sounding very sure.

Clint looked at the gun on Temple's hip. They never did establish whether or not the man could use it.

"No," Clint said, "I'll check it out."

"Alone?" Temple asked.

"No," Clint said, "you go and find the sheriff."

"But—"

"I'll go to the Red Queen," Clint said. "I have a feeling this all ties in together."

"You might be right," Mayor Stanley said. "I've long been aware that Ned was an ambitious man, with his eyes on my job. He may have gotten in way over his head."

Clint looked at the man's body and said, "I don't think there's much doubt about that, Mr. Mayor."

FORTY-FOUR

The Red Queen was just what Clint thought it would be. From the street he could hear the loud voices, and the music—a bad piano player on a piano that had bad keys.

All he had to go on was the sketch that Leo from the livery had done. On the other hand, he knew the killer knew what he looked like. He probably should have waited for Temple to show up with the sheriff, but if all of this was connected—and he refused to accept any hint of coincidence—then Tanner might be inside, with the killer.

He mounted the boardwalk and went through the batwings.

The mayor was helpful, and told Temple where Sheriff Evans lived. He pounded on the door, which was answered by an older woman, who didn't look happy.

"Why are you bangin' on our door?" she demanded.

"I need the sheriff, ma'am."

"What for? Ain't Abilene's police department good enough for you? You have to bother my husband after hours?"

"Who is it, Julia?" Evans's voice shouted from inside.

"It's Harry Temple, Sheriff!" Temple shouted. "Clint Adams is in trouble."

Julia Evans stood aside as her husband charged out the door, fully dressed and wearing his gun.

"Well, lad, come on," he said. "Let's go get the man out of trouble."

As they hurried from the house, Temple said, "Sorry I interrupted your dinner."

"Son," Evans said, "you probably saved my stomach . . ."

Clint entered the saloon. The commotion inside kept him from being noticed by many except those who were seated right near the door.

As the men turned to look at him, he studied their faces. None matched the sketch.

He walked to the bar.

The killer noticed Clint Adams through the commotion because he was watching for him. Seated across from him was the editor, Pete Tanner. Bruised and battered, but alive and afraid to move.

Tanner also saw Clint. The killer looked across at him over the shoulder of the saloon girl sitting in his lap.

"Relax, Mr. Tanner," he said. "It's almost over."

He caressed the girl's slim neck while he moved his gaze to a table of three men. He jerked his head toward the bar and nodded.

"Are we really gonna do this?" Lenny Copper asked.

Mick Lynch looked at him and said, "Fella says Beaumont is payin'. And when the district attorney is payin', we're doin'."

"Yeah," Eric Markey said, "it's the Gunsmith."

"They say this is the time to take him," Lynch said. "They say he's slowed down. Come on, boys. Let's make a name for ourselves."

They stood up.

* * *

Clint ordered a beer, but didn't drink it. Aside from the fact
that there was something floating in it, he saw in the mirror
behind the bar that three men were rising from their table.
And he saw Tanner. Across from the bruised editor sat a
man with a girl in his lap. The girl hid his face—for the
moment.

As the three men moved toward Clint, it quickly became
apparent to the patrons of the Red Queen that something
was up. They grew quiet and moved aside. Clint turned to
face the men, and now it was dead quiet.

"You men getting paid enough for this?" Clint asked.

"We're doin' okay, Mr. Gunsmith," Mick Lynch said.
"How are you doin' tonight?" He was standing between
his partners.

"I'd be doing better if I wasn't faced with the prospect
of killing three fools."

The man on either side of the middle one flinched, but
not him.

"Who are you working for?" Clint asked.

"Now that don't much matter, does it?"

Clint had an idea, decided to deal it out and see how it
played.

"Wouldn't happen to be the district attorney, would it?"
Clint asked. "Did he send word with another man?"

One of the other men risked a glance over his shoulder
at the table where Tanner was sitting, across from a man
Clint still couldn't see.

"Afraid you fellows are unemployed," Clint said. "Your
boss is dead. In fact, he was killed by the very fellow who
brought you the job. So—"

"Fuck this," Mick Lynch said, and drew.

At least, he tried to draw. But he was dead before he
could even touch his gun. Clint drew cleanly and shot him
once in the chest. Then he holstered his gun.

"He just died for free," Clint told the other two. "How about you two?"

The two men stared down at their partner, then they both shook their heads and ran for the batwings, leaving them flapping in their wake.

Clint walked over to the table and said to the editor, "Take it easy, Mr. Tanner."

Then he looked at the killer, who grinned at him over the young girl. She was now sure she was someplace she didn't want to be. The man's smile revealed yellowed teeth, probably from years of smoking. He appeared to be in his fifties, and who knew how long he'd been killing women?

"I gotta get to work—" she started, but the killer tightened his arm around her waist.

"Stay where you are, darlin'," he said with an Irish accent.

"Mulligan," Clint said. "Is that your real name after all?"

"That it is, laddie," Mulligan said.

"Well, Mr. Mulligan," Clint said, "you might as well let the girl go. It's all over."

"Not quite," Mulligan said. He brought his other hand around and pressed the blade of his knife to the girl's throat.

"Come on now," Clint said, "that's the way you kill men, isn't it?"

"Sometimes."

"And sometimes you even shoot at men from a distance for sport. Like you shot at my friend and me?"

"Aye," Mulligan said, grinning again.

"So this knife isn't your style. You strangle women. You like killing them with an orange scarf for some reason."

"You ain't leavin' me much choice here, lad," Mulligan said. "Come on, girl, get up slow."

They got to their feet, and the blade never left the tender flesh of her throat. Her eyes were wide with fright.

"We're leavin'," Mulligan said, and started backing

away. "You better make sure we got a clear path to the door."

"Clear out," Clint said to the men behind the killer. "Give him room."

Mulligan started backing toward the door, pulling the girl with him. Clint was waiting for any opening, and when Temple came through the batwings, Clint almost yelled at him to watch out, but instead kept quiet. The young reporter had waited two years for this.

As Mulligan pulled the girl back toward him, Temple drew his gun, reversed it, and slammed the butt down on the top of the killer's head with as much force as he could muster. The man dropped the knife and slumped to the floor. The girl scampered away. Evans came in behind Temple and stared down at the man.

"Did I kill him?" Temple asked.

Evans checked.

"Nope, he's still breathin'."

"The arrest is yours, Sheriff," Clint said. "Mr. Tanner will testify that he's the killer."

Evans looked at the other man on her floor.

"I killed him," Clint said. "Fair fight."

"I'll bet," Evans said. "Come on, I need a coupla fellas to carry this man—what's his name?"

"Mulligan."

"Really?" Temple asked.

Clint nodded.

"Some of you boys help me get Mr. Mulligan to my jail," Evans said. He looked at Clint. "This ain't gonna make the mayor and the chief happy."

"Maybe the mayor won't be mayor much longer, Sheriff," Clint said.

Evans nodded his thanks as three men dragged Mulligan from the saloon.

"Gents," Tanner said, coming up behind them, "drinks are on me."

"Not here," Clint said. "Let's go to the Big Horn—if you're feeling up to it."

"Just a few bruises," Tanner said. "Nothing a whiskey won't cure. And then, boy," he said to Temple, "we got a story to write—and I got a permanent job I wanna offer you."

Clint looked at Temple, who smiled and said, "Why not?"

Watch for

DEADLY FORTUNE

398th novel in the exciting GUNSMITH series

from Jove

Coming in February!

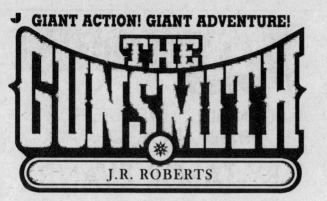

GIANT ACTION! GIANT ADVENTURE!

THE GUNSMITH

J.R. ROBERTS

LONGARM

GIANT-SIZED ADVENTURE FROM AVENGING ANGEL LONGARM.

BY TABOR EVANS

penguin.com/actionwesterns

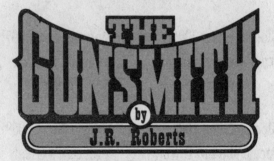